THE NIGHT BEFORE CHRISTMAS

Just as Jessica felt herself drifting off, a sharp sound made her whole body start. She stared into the darkness. The room seemed even blacker than usual—the night light in the bathroom must have gone out. Jessica shivered.

She felt disoriented. What time was it? She turned to look at her digital clock. The blue numerals read 12:00.

Midnight. The witching hour, when strange things happened.

Jessica felt her bed shake slightly.

Her heart seemed to jump into her throat. Too frightened to shriek, she turned slowly to look. What she saw made her draw back in horror.

A little girl stood at the foot of her bed.

"Who are you?" Jessica gulped.

The child smiled. "I am the Ghost of Christmas Past."

SWEET VALLEY TWINS
◇ SUPER CHILLER ◇

The Christmas Ghost

Written by
Jamie Suzanne

Created by
FRANCINE PASCAL

A BANTAM SKYLARK BOOK®
NEW YORK · TORONTO · LONDON · SYDNEY · AUCKLAND

RL 4, 008-012

THE CHRISTMAS GHOST
A Bantam Skylark Book / December 1989

*Sweet Valley High® and Sweet Valley Twins are trademarks of
Francine Pascal*

Conceived by Francine Pascal

*Produced by Daniel Weiss Associates, Inc.
33 West 17th Street,
New York, NY 10011*

Cover art by James Mathewuse

*Skylark Books is a registered trademark of Bantam Books, a division of
Bantam Doubleday Dell Publishing Group, Inc.
Registered in U.S. Patent and Trademark Office and elsewhere.*

ISBN 0-553-15767-1

Published simultaneously in the United States and Canada

PRINTED IN THE UNITED STATES OF AMERICA

0 9 8 7 6 5 4 3 2 1

One

◇

"Elizabeth, do you believe in ghosts?" twelve-year-old Jessica Wakefield asked her twin. She studied the movie poster in front of her. It showed a transparent figure hovering over some frightened children. Just looking at it gave Jessica the chills. *What would it be like to be haunted by a real ghost?* she thought. She reached for her sister's arm and squeezed tightly for an instant to assure herself that this was all make-believe.

"No, Jess, I don't believe in ghosts," Elizabeth replied, pulling her sister gently away from the poster. "Ghosts only exist in movies and books. Oh, look at this," she said, moving over to the next store window.

Jessica quickly followed. The two girls had stopped by the Sweet Valley Mall after school to look at the holiday decorations.

"Look at that gorgeous blue sweater," Jessica exclaimed with a dreamy look on her face. "I'd love to get that for Christmas. Oh, Lizzie, I just can't wait for Christmas to come."

"Me neither," Elizabeth agreed. "This is my favorite time of year."

Jessica smiled broadly. "Only one more week of school, then we'll be out for the holiday break. How are we ever going to wait that long?"

"If you spend any more time window-shopping, it'll be Christmas before we leave the mall," Elizabeth said, giggling.

"Doesn't the mall look wonderful?" Jessica asked. "Look at the big silver snowflakes hanging everywhere. And the giant Christmas tree in the center. And look, there's Santa's house."

"I remember when we used to wait in line forever to see Santa," Elizabeth told her twin, laughing at the memory. "When we were three, you threw a tantrum and refused to sit on Santa's lap because his beard scared you."

"You can't possibly remember that." Jessica

turned to look at her sister. "That was ages ago."

"Well, I've heard Mom tell the story often enough," Elizabeth admitted. "Oh, look at this," she exclaimed.

The girls hurried to the next storefront. "I like the purse with the silver buckle," Elizabeth told her sister.

"I think the purple one with the gold braid is prettier," Jessica decided. "I'd love someone to give me that."

Elizabeth smiled. "You'd look like a gypsy. And if that's a hint, you're too late. I've already bought and wrapped your Christmas present."

Jessica grinned at her twin. It was just like looking into a mirror. The girls were identical from their blue-green eyes and long, silky blond hair to the dimple in their left cheeks.

But in spite of their identical appearance, the twins were very different inside. Jessica loved being the center of attention, and her favorite activities usually involved the Unicorn Club, an exclusive group of pretty, popular girls who thought they were unique. In fact, they thought of themselves as being so special that they always wore something purple, the color of royalty. Jessica and her friends spent most of their time discussing the latest fashion, the cutest boys, and the theme of their next party.

Elizabeth had her own group of friends, who were much more interested in school-related activities. Not only did Elizabeth secretly think that the Unicorns were boring, but she thought they were snobby, as well. She found it much more challenging to write for the sixth-grade school newspaper and found great comfort in curling up with a good mystery novel. Her biggest dream was to be a writer someday.

Once in a while, the girls' differences led to quarrels, but usually the twins were the best of friends. Today both girls were in a good mood, as if they both felt the same overflowing of good spirits that Christmastime can bring.

"What did you get me? Can you give me a little hint?" Jessica's tone was playful.

Elizabeth shook her head firmly. "Surprises are the best part of Christmas," she told her sister.

"Speak for yourself," Jessica said. "Anyhow, whatever you got me, I just hope it's purple. You know that purple is—"

"Your favorite color," Elizabeth finished for her twin. "How could I forget?"

Linking arms, the girls wandered to the next shop. This window display held a fat spruce tree, twinkling with small white lights and hung with white-and-silver ornaments.

Jessica pressed her nose to the window, surveying the gifts displayed under the tree. She couldn't wait to open all her own presents on Christmas morning. How was she going to be able to wait that long?

"Oh, look at that gold bracelet," Jessica exclaimed. "The one with the heart-shaped charm. Isn't it pretty?"

"It is pretty," Elizabeth agreed. "But it looks very expensive."

"And that miniature teddy bear," Jessica added. "Isn't it sweet? This is the best store yet."

"Hey, Jess, we've got to go or we'll miss our bus," Elizabeth said, looking at her watch. "I didn't know it was so late. I told Amy and Julie I'd meet them at our house at four-thirty. We have to go over the final plans for the holiday bazaar."

"But I'm not ready to leave yet," Jessica said. "We haven't even been to the second level."

"I know, Jess, but Amy and Julie are waiting for me." As Elizabeth headed for the nearest exit with Jessica trailing behind, something caught her eye. She sighed.

"Oh, Jess, look, over there. Isn't that porcelain carousel horse beautiful?" She spoke in a whisper and pointed at the delicate miniature sculpture.

"Oh, Lizzie. That is gorgeous," Jessica agreed. "And it has a purple harness—my favorite color."

Both girls pressed close to the window to get a better look.

"What a beautiful white mane. And look at all the colors in its trim," Elizabeth murmured. "Like jewels. It reminds me of the merry-go-round in the park. Remember how often we used to ride it when we were small?"

Jessica nodded. "You cried when they tore it down," she recalled. "It does remind me of the horses on the old carousel."

"Only this is better." Elizabeth took a deep breath. "Look at the gleam in its eye. This horse looks almost alive, ready to fly right off the carousel."

"Why don't you add it to your Christmas list?" Jessica suggested, feeling just a tinge of envy. She wouldn't mind having the pretty horse for her own room.

Elizabeth shook her head. "I've already asked for a lot of things," she said. "And this horse is probably expensive."

Jessica felt relieved, but she only said, "At

least Steven didn't say that your Christmas list is long enough to wrap around the house ten times, like he did about mine."

Elizabeth grinned. Steven was the twins' fourteen-year-old brother. "You know Steven likes to tease you, Jess. Don't pay any attention to him."

Jessica stared at the horse again. "I like the horse, too. It's awfully pretty."

"Come on, we really have to go now," Elizabeth urged her sister.

They ran for the nearest mall exit.

It was only a short bus ride home, but they managed to discuss all the wonderful things they'd seen at the mall.

"I don't know which one I'd rather have," Jessica said. "That blue sweater or the gold bracelet or—"

"The carousel horse was the best," Elizabeth said, sighing at the thought. "That's a really special gift for someone."

Jessica seemed to change her mind instantly. "You're right," she agreed. "The carousel horse was the best."

As they approached the front door, Elizabeth saw two familiar faces peeking around the doorway.

"Hey, Elizabeth, what happened? We've

been waiting for ages," Amy Sutton said, pushing her thin blond hair out of her eyes and frowning.

Behind her, Julie Porter nodded agreement. "I have to be home at five-thirty," she said. "That doesn't leave us much time."

Jessica had already disappeared into the kitchen.

"Sorry," Elizabeth said. "We got so carried away window-shopping at the mall that I lost track of the time. Come on up to my room."

She headed to the staircase, and the other two girls followed her up to her bedroom. Julie and Amy sat down on the bed, and Elizabeth sat down at her desk. She instantly pulled her notebook out of her bag and got ready to start writing.

"Any more contributions for our holiday bazaar?" Elizabeth asked. She looked from Amy to Julie. Sweet Valley Middle School was holding a bazaar to help raise money for a new piece of equipment for the children's wing of the local hospital. Elizabeth, Amy, and Julie were in charge of collecting contributions for the sale. They hoped to raise at least a hundred dollars on Saturday.

"I got some more clothes," Amy announced.

"And an old stereo. It's a little scratched up, but it still works."

Elizabeth added the items to her list.

"I collected a used bike and two boxes of old toys," Julie added. "I hope we make lots of money."

Elizabeth nodded. "Me, too. I want our fund-raising drive to be a big success. Wouldn't it be great if we could make more money than the high school?"

They all grinned at the idea.

"I don't know, though," Amy cautioned. "I hear the high school is having a gift-wrapping booth right in the center of the mall. They'll probably make lots of money with that."

Julie sounded more optimistic. "Just wait till the people taste the cookies we're going to bake for the bazaar on Saturday. When they find out what good cooks we are, we'll rake the money in."

"At least we're not selling old cookies to go with the old clothes," Amy joked. "And remember we'll be selling those ornaments we made in art class. My mom promised to come, and I know she'll buy something."

Elizabeth smiled. "I just hope our mothers aren't our only customers. Don't forget to remind all your friends and neighbors about the bazaar, too. We'll need a big turnout to make it work."

Just before five-thirty, Elizabeth walked her friends down to the front door. As she turned to go back upstairs, she couldn't help overhearing Jessica talking to their mother in the kitchen.

"You should have seen it, Mom. It was the most beautiful carousel horse I've ever seen. I'd really love to find it in one of my Christmas packages."

"Along with the other three dozen items you've already asked for?" Mrs. Wakefield teased gently. "Are you sure you want the horse, Jessica? It sounds to me more like something Elizabeth would like."

"Oh, no," Jessica said clearly. "Elizabeth didn't like the horse at all. Please, Mom, can't you get it for me?"

"Well, we'll see," Mrs. Wakefield said. "There should be a few surprises under the tree."

Elizabeth felt a sharp rush of surprise and disappointment. Her cheeks felt hot. How could Jessica tell such a deliberate lie? Elizabeth had made it clear that she liked the horse. And she had been the one to spot it in the first place.

Jessica must really want the horse badly to lie

like that, Elizabeth thought. She walked slowly into the kitchen.

"Hello, dear. Dinner's almost ready. Why don't both of you set the table tonight?" Mrs. Wakefield smiled at them.

"OK," Elizabeth said. "Come on, Jess. Let's use the special Santa place mats."

"Right. And the red candles, and the sprigs of holly," Jessica said.

The twins walked into the dining room and began to set the table with all the holiday trimmings. Elizabeth put her disturbing thoughts aside and began to feel better. She was determined that this Christmas would be the best ever!

Two

◇

On Friday afternoon, Elizabeth hurried home from school. She found her mother in the kitchen with an apron tied around her waist.

"Oh, I'm glad you're here," Elizabeth said, giving her mother a quick hug. "I was afraid you might have forgotten that we'd planned to bake cookies for the holiday bazaar tomorrow."

"I wouldn't forget something as important as that," Mrs. Wakefield said, smiling at her daughter. "I've got everything ready."

Elizabeth washed her hands and put on an apron to keep her clothes clean. She surveyed the counter, already covered with canisters of flour and sugar and small bottles of spices. Tubes of icing were laid out and several cookie pans were stacked on the stove top.

"This is going to be fun," Elizabeth said. She sat down at the table and began to flip through her favorite cookbook. "Which recipe shall we start with?"

"You girls always like sugar cookies," Mrs. Wakefield pointed out. "And they can be decorated many different ways."

"Good idea," Elizabeth said. "Do we still have the Christmas cookie cutters?"

"Of course." Her mother pulled open a kitchen drawer and searched for the holiday cookie cutters. "Here we are. A snowman, a reindeer, a star, a Christmas tree, and Santa himself."

Elizabeth grinned. "That's great, Mom. I'll start sifting the flour now and you can—"

"What happened to Jessica?" Mrs. Wakefield cut in as she began to grease the cookie sheets. "I thought she was going to help bake cookies, too."

"I saw her talking to Lila Fowler on the school steps," Elizabeth explained. "I was in a hurry to get home, so I didn't wait for her."

Just then, the front door banged. Jessica appeared in the kitchen doorway, her hair slightly windblown. She was panting, as if she'd run the last few blocks. "Hi, Mom, Lizzie. I'm going over to Lila's house to help her make plans for the big Christmas party. Just think! Only a week and two days till Christmas."

"I thought you were going to help with the cookies," Elizabeth reminded her sister. She couldn't help feeling a little bit hurt. "The party's not until next Wednesday. You've got lots of time to get ready."

Jessica shrugged. "Oh, you'll do fine without me," she assured her sister. "Besides, you're a much better cook than I am. And Lila really needs my help."

"Sure, all alone in that big house with only a housekeeper to help her," Elizabeth murmured, shaking her head. But still, she hated to dim Jessica's excitement.

"It's going to be such a great Christmas party," Jessica was saying now, her eyes shining. "And Lila needs my advice on the decorations. She knows what good taste I have."

Mrs. Wakefield nodded. "I'm sure you'll give her good advice," she agreed, smiling just a little.

"Decorating talent must run in the family," Jessica boasted.

Mrs. Wakefield laughed, and Elizabeth smiled.

Their mother worked part-time as an interior designer, and she was well known through Sweet Valley for her decorating skill.

After Jessica left, Elizabeth decided to forget about her sister's promise to help. Jessica frequently forgot about promises she had made when it interfered with something she wanted to do.

Elizabeth broke four eggs carefully into a large bowl, and beat the eggs until they were light and fluffy. Then she measured the shortening, sugar, and vanilla extract, and added some orange peel. Mrs. Wakefield measured the milk, then Elizabeth added the rest of the ingredients and mixed everything carefully.

"This should make a lot of cookies," Elizabeth told her mother. "We'll need plenty for the bazaar."

They divided the dough into four parts, and put the pieces into the refrigerator to chill for an hour.

"While we wait, we'll start some ginger snaps," Mrs. Wakefield suggested. "They can go straight into the oven."

The next few hours seemed to fly by. The sugar cookies were rolled out, cut into shapes, and baked, and then came the best part of all: deciding how to decorate them.

Elizabeth covered the stars with gold and silver sprinkles, gave the snowmen raisin eyes and chocolate grins, and used frosting to give Santa a red outfit and white beard.

When Steven came home from basketball practice, he was drawn immediately to the kitchen.

"Hey, something smells really good," he said, reaching for a cookie.

"No freebies," Elizabeth announced, hurrying to block his path. "These are for the holiday bazaar tomorrow."

"Don't you need someone to test them?" Steven pleaded, trying to look as pathetic as he could. "Someone who's about to die of starvation at your very feet?" He pretended to tremble as he fell to one knee.

Elizabeth giggled, but her tone was firm. "Nope. These are for paying customers only," she told him. "And besides, I know you. If you started testing, I'd have no more cookies left! Come to the bazaar tomorrow and buy some. In fact, bring the whole basketball team."

"No compassion," Steven told her, shaking his head. He settled for a glass of milk and a slice of chocolate cake from the refrigerator, then headed for his room.

A little later, Mr. Wakefield arrived home

from his law office. With his briefcase still under his arm, he looked into the kitchen, too.

"Smells like Mrs. Santa's workshop," he told them cheerfully. "And it looks like someone's been working awfully hard in here." He nodded toward the tableful of rows and rows of cookies.

Elizabeth gave her dad a floury hug. "Don't the cookies look good?"

"Scrumptious," Mr. Wakefield agreed. "In fact, I'd better leave right now, or temptation may prove too much for me."

It took Elizabeth until dinnertime to finish decorating. She couldn't help thinking that the work would have gone much faster if Jessica had been there to help her.

While Mrs. Wakefield put hamburger patties on the grill, Elizabeth finished the last batch of cookies, then wrapped individual packages and tied each packet with a bright red bow.

"I'm ready for the bazaar," she told herself. "I just hope we make lots and lots of money!"

On Saturday morning, Elizabeth was ready early, but once again Jessica begged off.

"I'm just too tired to get up yet," she explained in a groggy voice. "Lila and I worked hard yesterday, and I need my sleep." Jessica ignored Elizabeth's frown and burrowed quickly back under the covers.

Elizabeth sighed, then hurried down to help her dad load the van with all her goodies.

When they reached the middle school grounds, Julie, Amy, Brooke Dennis, and Nora Mercandy were all there to help. They set up the displays, and the tables were soon crowded with customers. Elizabeth saw her mom, as well as Julie's mother and Brooke's dad, among the people selecting cookies and holiday items to buy.

Other classmates brought more cookies to add to the tables, and handmade Christmas and Hanukkah decorations to sell.

"How much do you think we made?" Amy asked at the end of the afternoon as she helped Brooke take down their signs. "The money box looked really full. Were you keeping count, Elizabeth?"

"I was, but I lost track after the first hour. Let's hurry up and put everything away so we can start counting the money," Elizabeth said.

"Why don't we go to your house when we're done and count the money there?" Amy suggested.

"Good idea," Elizabeth said. "My house is the closest." Everyone else nodded in agreement.

On the walk back to the Wakefield house,

Elizabeth carefully carried the cash box, making sure no money slipped out.

"How did it go, girls?" Mrs. Wakefield asked as they marched through the front door one by one.

"We haven't counted our money yet," Elizabeth explained. "I'm keeping my fingers crossed."

"We worked hard, though," Julie said. "We did our best."

"I know. All those cookies we sold, and I didn't taste a single one." Amy sighed at the thought.

Mrs. Wakefield poured them each a glass of lemonade. "Don't worry. I just happen to have some very special cookies I bought this morning," she told them, winking at Elizabeth.

The girls laughed as they reached eagerly to sample their own baking.

"Umm, I knew my gingerbread men would turn out well," Julie said. "How much money have we got, Elizabeth?"

"Sshh, I'm counting," Elizabeth said. She arranged the stack of dollar bills, piled the coins in neat rows, and counted it twice to be sure.

"Forty-seven dollars and thirty-five cents," she announced finally.

"Well," Amy said. "That's pretty good, considering we couldn't charge very much for each bag of cookies."

"I know. But we had a goal of a hundred dollars," Elizabeth reminded her friends. "We still need to raise more than half of that. And I don't know what else to do to make more money. Any ideas?"

"What else do you think we could do, Elizabeth?" Julie asked.

"I'm not sure," Elizabeth admitted. They discussed ideas for another half-hour, then the other girls gathered their things to go.

"Don't be discouraged, Elizabeth," Amy said as she walked out the door. "We'll think of something. I know we will."

Elizabeth wasn't as confident as her friend. "I hope so," she said, waving goodbye. But right now, no one had any ideas.

Three

Sunday afternoon Elizabeth sat at her desk in her bedroom. She tried to concentrate on the paper in front of her, but her mind kept wandering.

"This is no way for the editor to behave," she scolded herself out loud. "This is the last article for the holiday edition of *The Sweet Valley Sixers*. I want it to be good!"

But she still found it hard to concentrate. She kept remembering how she wanted to come up with more ideas for the hospital fund-raising drive. No matter how long Elizabeth pondered, she just couldn't think of a really good plan.

A muffled sound across the hall distracted her. She stood up and slowly crept to her doorway.

Who was in her parents' bedroom? Mr. and Mrs. Wakefield had gone shopping together. Probably for Christmas gifts, since they had discouraged Jessica's request to ride along with them to the mall.

There it came again! Elizabeth felt her skin prickle with goose bumps. What was making that noise? Someone or something was definitely in her parents' bedroom.

Jessica had gone outside, and Steven was at the park. Could it be a burglar? Should she dial 911? But the upstairs telephone was presently in her parents' bedroom. She'd have to sneak down the stairs to reach another phone, and hope the unknown intruder didn't hear her.

Another slight rustle made her stiffen. Elizabeth tiptoed into the hall. She hesitated, then crept closer to the bedroom doorway. Taking a deep breath, she eased around the slightly open door and peeked inside.

"Jessica! What are you doing?" she exclaimed.

Jessica whirled, her face slightly flushed. "Lizzie! You scared me to death."

"Serves you right for poking around in

Mom's stuff," Elizabeth told her sister. She frowned at her twin. "What are you up to, anyhow? Looking for your Christmas presents already?"

"Of course not. Mom said I could borrow her silver chain," Jessica said. But she didn't quite meet her sister's eye.

Elizabeth wasn't convinced. "Even so, you know perfectly well her chain is in her jewelry box, not in the bottom of the closet."

"Well, I was trying on her high heels. After all, I'll probably be wearing heels before too long," Jessica added. "I thought I might need some practice."

Elizabeth shook her head. "Come on, Jessica. I'm not that gullible. You were snooping, and you know it!"

Jessica's face turned even redder. "I was not. You're always jumping to conclusions. Just because I accidentally happened to find some packages—"

Elizabeth sighed. "I knew it. If Mom and Dad find out that you were poking around in their room—"

"Oh, come on," Jessica coaxed. "Don't be such a spoilsport. Look what I found."

Before Elizabeth could stop her, Jessica

picked up the nearest shopping bag and held it open so Elizabeth could see what was inside.

"The carousel horse!" Elizabeth's eyes widened. "I wonder who it's for."

"For me, of course," Jessica declared, pulling it out of the bag and touching the smooth porcelain horse. "I asked for it. You decided you didn't want it."

Elizabeth swallowed hard. She felt a lump in her throat, and her eyes prickled. She hadn't said she didn't want it. But she nodded bravely. No point in arguing about it now.

"You'd better get out of here," Elizabeth warned. "Mom and Dad will be home soon."

Jessica carefully put the horse back into the shopping bag, and they both hurried out into the hall.

"I can't wait to see my other gifts," Jessica said.

Elizabeth couldn't bear to watch her twin gloating over the carousel horse. She walked slowly downstairs, and tried very hard not to think about it anymore.

In the family room, she found the weekend section of the newspaper scattered across the couch, where Jessica had left it.

Wondering if there were any good movies

on at the Valley Cinema, Elizabeth picked up the paper and scanned the headlines. She was still reading the paper when her parents came through the front door.

"Have any luck shopping?" she asked her mother.

"Yes, we found a few things, but the crowds are terrible," Mrs. Wakefield said. She piled her parcels on the hall table. "I need a snack. Would you like something to drink, Elizabeth?"

"Sure, Mom," Elizabeth said, still eyeing the paper. Then she jumped to her feet, feeling a thrill of excitement.

"Wow, Mom! Listen to this."

Four

◇

"What is it, dear?" Mrs. Wakefield asked.

"This is incredible," Elizabeth said. She jumped up from the couch, waving the newspaper over her head as if it were a flag. "You won't believe it. Beau Dillon is coming to Sweet Valley!"

"Who?"

"You know," Elizabeth reminded her mother. "Beau Dillon, the movie star. He's seventeen and he's such a good actor. We saw him in a movie at the mall last month."

"Oh, yes." Mrs. Wakefield nodded. "I remember him. Why is he coming here?"

"He's doing interviews to publicize his new

movie, *Tender Hearts*. It's about a teenager who gets cancer and almost dies. I've got an incredible idea!''

Mrs. Wakefield sat down on the couch, her expression interested. ''Yes?''

Elizabeth took a deep breath, barely able to contain her excitement. ''This article says Beau spent a lot of time in children's hospitals researching his role in the new movie. He's done fund-raising events several times since then, because he got so interested in helping sick kids. I bet if I write to him, he'd help with a fund-raiser for us. Then we'd be sure to raise enough money for the new equipment at the children's wing of the hospital.''

Elizabeth could just imagine how much money they'd make with Beau's help. They'd make even more than their goal. It would be the most successful fund-raiser ever. But to her surprise, Mrs. Wakefield looked uncertain.

''What's wrong, Mom? Don't you think it's a good idea?''

''Yes,'' Mrs. Wakefield said. ''I think it's very good. I just don't want you to get your hopes up. You have to remember how busy actors are, Elizabeth. You don't know if he'll get your letter before he leaves for Sweet Valley, or if he'll have enough free time to plan his schedule around a new commitment. I wouldn't count on this just yet."

"Well, I think it's worth a try," Elizabeth said. "I just know Beau Dillon would want to help if he could. I'm going to write him a letter right now."

She hurried upstairs. In her bedroom, Elizabeth found a box of pale blue stationery. She sat down at her desk and composed her letter. She made it brief and to the point, but—she hoped—hard to resist.

Dear Mr. Dillon:

My name is Elizabeth Wakefield. My friends and I at Sweet Valley Middle School are trying to raise money to buy a new type of laser for the children's wing at Sweet Valley Hospital. Some very sick children need this new equipment for their treatment. We've worked hard but still haven't made enough money.

I know you're a very busy person, but if you would appear at a fund-raiser for us, I'm sure we could raise the money we need. Please, could you help us?

Sincerely,
Elizabeth Wakefield

Elizabeth made sure her address and phone number were printed plainly at the bottom of the paper. Then she found the name and address of Beau Dillon's studio in the newspaper article and addressed the envelope. She found a stamp in her desk drawer, then hurried downstairs.

She decided to run to the corner and put her letter in the mailbox. She didn't have any time to waste. She slipped the envelope into the big blue mailbox, crossing her fingers as it disappeared from sight. If only Beau received her letter in time—if only he was willing to help!

Elizabeth walked home slowly. When she reached the house, she went into the kitchen and found Steven in front of the refrigerator. His arms were filled with three packages of cold cuts and a jar of pickles.

"I saw you rush out of the house with that letter," Steven said. "What was it—a secret love letter?"

"Of course not." Elizabeth knew she must be turning pink. "Something much more important—a letter to Beau Dillon."

"Beau Dillon, the actor? Ha, I knew it. She's in love." Steven rolled his eyes and gave an exaggerated sigh. He began to put a mammoth sandwich together.

"No, no, smarty." Steven was a terrible

tease. "I'm asking for his help with the fund-raising drive for the hospital."

"A famous actor like that? You must be kidding. He'll probably never even see your letter. He must get bags and bags of fan mail. And even if he did, he'd never take the time for a place as small as Sweet Valley. Hollywood stars only do big-time events in big cities."

Elizabeth felt her heart sink. "Well, I think he might," she said bravely. "Did you read the weekend section of yesterday's paper?"

"What's that have to do with anything?" Steven mumbled with his mouth full.

"Beau's coming to Sweet Valley to do some publicity work," Elizabeth explained. "Besides, you don't know for sure that he wouldn't want to help."

"Wait and see," Steven said as he took another big bite of his sandwich. "You'll never hear from this guy. He's probably just another pretty face."

Elizabeth headed for her bedroom, hoping that her brother was wrong. She sat down at her desk again, feeling her enthusiasm fade. Well, if Beau didn't respond, what else could they do to raise money?

She thought about a car wash as a last resort, but she just sighed and went back to making notes.

* * *

The next few days were the busiest Elizabeth could remember. She and the rest of the staff finished the special edition of *The Sweet Valley Sixers* and celebrated with a party. Mr. Bowman, Elizabeth's English teacher and the paper's adviser, brought cupcakes he had baked himself, and everyone had a great time.

The holiday edition of the sixth-grade newspaper met with widespread approval. Everyone liked the Christmas and Hanukkah puzzles and thought the jokes were funny.

Then the middle school held a special holiday assembly Wednesday morning. First came a performance by the middle school choir. Jessica and Elizabeth took their places on stage with the rest of the singers. The girls wore red blouses and the boys green shirts, as they sang all their favorite Christmas carols. Elizabeth had a solo in "Silent Night," and although she'd practiced for two weeks, she still felt her stomach jump when she stood up to sing. But to her surprise, her voice sounded strong and clear, and Amy gave her the thumbs-up sign when she sat back down.

The choir received loud applause when they filed off the stage. As they took their seats with the rest of the audience, a juggler and a clown appeared. It was a wonderful holiday performance, and the crowd cheered wildly. When it was over, the middle school students were dismissed so they could get an early start on their vacation.

"Hooray!" Amy Sutton cried as she and Elizabeth hurried out of the building. "It was a great day, but I'm still glad to get out of school. I love the holidays. Just a few days left until Christmas!"

"I know," Elizabeth said. "It's been hard thinking about schoolwork this week. I'm so glad vacation is finally here!"

"I've got to get ready for the party tonight," Amy said. "My mom's going to braid my hair."

Elizabeth grinned. Amy was a tomboy and usually didn't spend much time worrying about her appearance. "You'll look great. I'm sure of it," she said.

"I hope so. I can't believe Lila Fowler invited the whole sixth grade to her Christmas party, instead of just the Unicorns and their friends."

Elizabeth nodded. "I think she hopes for extra Christmas presents," she confided to her friend.

"Want to come to my house and help me decide what to wear?"

Elizabeth shook her head. "I can't. I have to hurry home and check the mail."

"Expecting something special?"

"Maybe." Elizabeth didn't want to talk

about her secret plan just yet. What if Steven was right, and Beau never answered her letter?

"All right. I'll see you tonight, then," Amy said.

Elizabeth walked quickly toward home. When she got there, she hurried up the front walk to the mailbox. She pulled out a handful of cards and envelopes, raced through the front door, and dumped them all on the kitchen counter. Then she began to sort through the pile.

Christmas cards, bills—then a small envelope addressed to Elizabeth Wakefield!

Elizabeth's heart began to beat fast. She didn't recognize the handwriting, and the postmark read *Los Angeles*. Elizabeth clutched the envelope tightly, almost afraid to open it. What if Beau said no?

Unable to bear the suspense any longer, she ripped open the envelope. The note inside was short. She read the message slowly.

Dear Elizabeth,

Thanks for your letter. I'd like to support the children's section of the hospital. I'll be in Sweet Valley the day before Christmas doing an interview to publicize my new movie.

It's hard for me to have a private conversation in public. If it's all right with your parents, I can stop

by your house after my interview, about noon.
Then we can discuss our next step.

You can call my agent to confirm our meeting.

Best wishes,
Beau Dillon

The signature was written in a sprawling hand, and there was a phone number printed at the bottom of the note.

Elizabeth took a deep breath. Her dreams were coming true! She felt such a thrill of pure joy that she could hardly sit still.

"What's going on?" Jessica entered the house and noticed Elizabeth pacing endlessly. "You look as if you've just been given a million dollars."

"Even better!" Elizabeth waved her note in the air. "I just knew he was a good person. I knew he'd want to help. Oh, this is so incredible."

"What are you talking about?"

"Beau Dillon—he's coming to Sweet Valley. More than that, he's coming to our house."

"What?" Jessica lurched forward and tried to grab the letter. "Let me see. I don't believe it. Why would Beau Dillon come here? Did you win a contest or something?"

"Of course not. He's going to help us raise money for the hospital." Elizabeth couldn't stop grinning. "Oh, wait till I tell Mom and Dad."

"Are you sure this isn't a joke?" Jessica asked. "I mean, it seems hard to believe—a big star like Beau doing something as boring as fund-raising."

"He doesn't think it's boring, and nobody would joke about something so important," Elizabeth protested. "Oh, I have to call and tell him it's OK."

First she hurried upstairs to tell her mother the good news.

"Mom, guess what!"

"Hello, sweetheart. Home from school already? What's up?"

Elizabeth explained quickly. "It's all right, isn't it, if Beau Dillon comes to our house? I got his reply today and he said he'd help. I'm so excited."

"It certainly is," Mrs. Wakefield agreed. "I'm so glad he's willing to help. If he makes an appearance, that should make your fund-raising efforts go over the top."

Elizabeth grinned. "You bet. I've got to call and tell him it's OK."

She hurried to the phone.

"Wait for me," Jessica yelled, suddenly appearing at her side. "Maybe Beau will answer himself. Anyhow, I want to see what happens."

Elizabeth dialed the number at the bottom of the note. As she waited, listening to the ringing at the other end, Elizabeth remembered Jessica's earlier comment. This couldn't be a joke. That would be too cruel.

To her relief, a man answered in a business-like tone. "Four-Star Agency."

Jessica leaned close, trying to hear the other side of the conversation. Elizabeth identified herself and explained about Beau's note.

"Oh, yes. You're the girl from Sweet Valley. Fine, I'll make sure the appointment's on his calendar."

"Thank you very much. Please don't forget, it's very important," Elizabeth urged and then hung up.

"Is he coming?" Jessica squealed when Elizabeth got off the phone.

"Yes," Elizabeth told her. "His agent made a note of the date on his calendar."

Jessica jumped up and down, but Elizabeth was lost in her own thoughts. She was almost afraid to believe her good fortune. Elizabeth was sure this Christmas would be very special—one she would remember all her life.

Elizabeth headed for her bedroom, tucked the note carefully into the side of her mirror, and lay down on her bed.

"What are you wearing to the party tonight?" Jessica asked, bursting through the bathroom door that connected the girls' bedrooms. "I can't decide."

"Oh, my new red sweater and skirt, I guess," Elizabeth said absently.

"You're really sure that Beau will come?" Jessica still seemed to find Elizabeth's news hard to believe. "Tell me again what the man said."

"It's all true," Elizabeth repeated patiently. "I spoke to Beau's agent. He's going to put our meeting on Beau's calendar."

"I can't believe it. Beau Dillon coming to our very own house!" Jessica's expression was dreamy. "Wow, this is great. We'll be famous!"

"Hey, don't get carried away," Elizabeth warned. "It's nothing personal, you know. We're only going to discuss a fund-raiser for the children's wing of the hospital."

Jessica smiled blissfully. "But I can talk to him, too, can't I? I'm one of his biggest fans. And Lila and Janet would do anything to meet him and—"

"Hold on. We can't take up too much of his time," Elizabeth told her sister. "Remember, this meeting is business."

"Spoilsport," Jessica grumbled.

Five

◇

"Hurry up, Jessica," Elizabeth called. "I thought you wanted to get to Lila's party on time." Elizabeth couldn't wait to get there, either. She wanted to tell Amy and Julie and the other girls on the fund-raising committee her wonderful news about Beau. They'd be so surprised.

The door opened at last, and Jessica appeared in the doorway. She struck a pose for her sister's benefit. "Well? What do you think?"

Elizabeth was in no mood to boost her twin's ego any more. "Very nice," she said shortly. "Let's go. Dad's waiting to drive us to Lila's house."

Jessica looked disappointed. She wore a lavender sweater and black miniskirt with leggings and dangling earrings.

"I think I look great," she said. "You just don't have an eye for fashion, Lizzie."

Elizabeth shook her head as she headed down the stairs. "If you're coming with us, you'd better get a move on."

Jessica hurried to catch up.

When they reached the Fowler home, Elizabeth and Jessica both scrambled out of the car. "Thanks, Dad," Elizabeth said.

"I'll pick you up at ten-thirty," Mr. Wakefield called as he pulled out of the driveway.

Elizabeth pulled her jacket close around her and followed Jessica to the front door. The night air felt cool. Lights shone from inside the Fowlers' big Georgian house, and the girls could hear rock music blaring. It looked as if the party was already in full swing. Jessica rang the doorbell, then tapped her foot impatiently as she waited for the door to open.

When it did, Lila Fowler smiled at them. "Hi, Jessica. Hi, Elizabeth. Merry early Christmas. Come on in. Lots of people are already here. Do you like my new outfit?"

She was wearing an obviously expensive

peach-colored sweater and a short skirt with leggings.

Jessica nodded her approval. "Terrific," she agreed. "We're dressed almost alike. I told Lizzie this was the latest style. She just never pays attention to the important things."

While Jessica and Lila discussed clothes, Elizabeth slipped out of her jacket and gave it to the housekeeper. The young woman smiled and motioned her on toward the big room beyond.

The first thing Elizabeth noticed was the large number of kids, all dressed in their best clothes. Most of the sixth grade had already arrived. The second thing to catch her eye was the big Christmas tree, whose top touched the high ceiling of the room. The tree was draped with lacy garlands and carefully hung with antique pink-and-gold ornaments.

The Wakefield tree, at home, was not as perfect or as spectacular, Elizabeth thought, but she liked it better. Instead of matched ornaments, their tree always featured the awkward cardboard bell Steven had made in first grade, and the odd-shaped clay reindeer the twins had constructed in kindergarten art class by themselves. And their store-bought ornaments had been selected one at a time over the years. Yes, she preferred her family's tree, Elizabeth decided.

Dozens of scarlet and white poinsettias brightened the corners of the room, and bows of holly hung along the walls. The big chandelier was draped in mistletoe. Elizabeth giggled as she saw how the boys all avoided being caught underneath the "kissing" plant.

She caught sight of Amy waving at her from across the room. Elizabeth hurried through the crowd to speak to her friend.

"Hi!" Amy said. "Isn't this great?" She motioned to the decorations all around the room, and the table laden with a variety of dishes. "The food is wonderful, too."

"Hi, Amy. Your hair looks terrific," Elizabeth said.

Amy's thin blond hair was pulled up in an elaborate French braid. She beamed at the praise. "Thanks. It took my mother almost half-an-hour to get it just right. It was so hard to stand still for that long—you may never see it this way again!"

Julie came up to join them. "Try the little pizzas," she told them. "They're great. And the cucumber dip is delicious."

"Just don't wait too long," Amy added, giggling. "The boys are already digging in."

Elizabeth laughed. "Good advice," she agreed.

"But listen to this. You'll never guess what happened!"

"What?" The girls looked interested.

"Our fund-raising problems are solved," Elizabeth told them. "We're going to make tons and tons of money for the children's wing of the hospital."

Amy looked a little skeptical. "We are? I wouldn't be too sure."

"No, really," Elizabeth interrupted. "This is something big. I didn't want to tell you until I knew for sure, but now I can. We're going to have a special fund-raiser with a big star."

"Huh?" Julie didn't seem convinced. "Don't tell me your brother is trying out his Harlem Globetrotter imitations again? If he puts the ball through the gym window, we'll owe more money than we make in admissions."

Elizabeth giggled. "Of course not." Steven was a good basketball player, especially for a freshman, but his attempts to do fancy tricks didn't always work. "I mean a big Hollywood star."

"Who?"

"Beau Dillon. Is that big enough for you?" Elizabeth replied, nearly bursting with pride.

"Beau Dillon!" Amy shrieked. "You're joking."

Her excited exclamation attracted attention

from the others around them. First Brooke Dennis came closer to hear what was happening. Then more kids followed, until almost everyone at the party was listening.

"What's this about Beau Dillon?" Caroline Pearce asked. She was the biggest gossip at the middle school. She had obviously managed to overhear part of their conversation, and now she was very curious.

"He's coming to Sweet Valley to do publicity interviews for his next movie," Elizabeth explained.

"*Tender Hearts*, the one about the boy with cancer," Brooke put in. "I read about that. It's supposed to be very good."

"I wrote him a letter," Elizabeth explained. "Because I'd read in an article that he became interested in helping sick kids while doing research for his movie. He sounded like a nice person. And—"

"And he's coming to *our* house the day before Christmas," Jessica interrupted, thrusting herself into the center of the crowd. "Isn't it thrilling? We'll get to talk to a real star."

"We?" Elizabeth asked. She couldn't help feeling a little bit annoyed.

"Of course," Jessica smiled. "You know I want to help you with the fund-raiser for the hospital. I wouldn't let my sister do all the work herself."

Since when had Jessica become so interested in the fund-raising drive, Elizabeth wondered. Could it be ever since a handsome movie star decided to help them?

"Honestly, Jess," she began.

But Jessica had already taken over the conversation. "I'm one of his biggest fans," she told the crowd. "I've seen all his movies, most of them two or three times. I can't wait till he comes. We'll have lots to talk about."

"Boy, this is so exciting," Ellen Riteman breathed. "Beau Dillon!"

"Jessica, you're so lucky," Tamara Chase added. "I'd die if Beau Dillon were coming to my house."

"The only thing we're talking about is the fund-raiser for the children's wing of the hospital," Elizabeth cut in.

"Well, he can't mind a few questions from an adoring fan." Jessica smiled sweetly at her sister.

"Come on," Lila said, her expression angry. "You really believe all this?"

Lila stood outside the group. She looked annoyed that everyone had forgotten about her and the party. Instead, everyone seemed interested in Elizabeth and Jessica and their big news.

"What do you mean by that?" Jessica said, frowning at her friend.

"Well, a big Hollywood star, and he just happens to want to drop in at your house?" Lila made the whole thing sound ridiculous.

A couple of the others began to look skeptical, too.

"Are you sure, Elizabeth?" Caroline asked. "Is he really coming? You're not just making this up?"

"I wouldn't make up something as important as this!" Elizabeth said quickly. "He's a nice person, that's all. Big stars don't have to be mean and selfish."

"Yes, but it is surprising," Ellen murmured. "Beau Dillon at your own house?"

"I have his note," Elizabeth defended herself.

"Oh, did you bring it with you?" Lila asked, sounding a little too sweet.

Elizabeth felt her cheeks burn and knew she was blushing. "Why should I carry it around with me?" she demanded. "It's at home on my bureau. But I did get the note, and I even called his agent, like he told me to. Beau Dillon is coming the day before Christmas, and then we'll make plans for a fund-raiser."

Elizabeth looked at Jessica, waiting for her to confirm her story, but Jessica remained silent.

"*If* he shows up," Lila said, her tone cool. "With all he has to do, how can Beau Dillon be interested in a silly middle school charity drive?"

"It's not silly," Elizabeth snapped.

"That's right," Amy put in. "Elizabeth knows what she's talking about. You wait and see, Lila."

"Ha. I'll believe it when I see him here," Lila said, her expression still skeptical.

"You'll see all right," Elizabeth muttered.

Beau will too show up, Elizabeth thought. *And then Lila will have to eat her words.*

On her way home, Elizabeth didn't say much, although Jessica talked merrily to their father. When they walked into the house, Mrs. Wakefield called, "How was the party, girls?"

"Very nice," Elizabeth said.

"Terrific," Jessica bubbled. "You should have seen all the decorations. I was the one who thought of getting the poinsettias! And we had mistletoe on the ceiling, but we couldn't seem to get the boys close enough—"

"Smart guys," Steven observed, grinning.

Jessica only giggled. "And the food was great," she told them. "We had these little pizzas, and tacos, and—"

Elizabeth headed for the staircase. She'd been more upset by Lila's ridicule than she wanted to admit. She certainly wasn't in the mood to listen to Jessica babble on about Lila's party.

Later, Jessica thrust her head around the bathroom door and spoke to her sister again.

"Didn't you have a good time? I sure did. And won't it be exciting when Beau comes to our house? I can't wait."

Elizabeth was buttoning her nightgown, but she turned quickly to stare at her sister. "I don't believe you," she exclaimed. "You didn't seem sure that Beau was coming when we were at the party. Why didn't you say something? You heard me call Beau's agent. You knew that I got his letter!"

Jessica shrugged. "I didn't want to get Lila mad at me," she admitted. "I think she's getting me something really good for Christmas. If she's angry, she might give my gift to Ellen instead."

Elizabeth bit her lip. This was too much. "I think you acted really awful," she told her sister. "Honestly, Jessica. If you keep on being so selfish, you'll end up with no friends at all."

Jessica looked outraged. "What a thing to

say! I'm not selfish. And I've got lots of friends. What about all the Unicorns? Everybody at school likes me. You take that back."

Elizabeth was too tired to argue. "Have it your way. Good night, Miss Popularity," she muttered, flipping the light switch.

Jessica retreated through the bathroom to her own bedroom, still muttering angrily.

On Christmas Eve day, Elizabeth woke early. It was the day Beau Dillon was coming, and Elizabeth was so excited that she had hardly slept the night before. Then, after his visit, she and Amy and the rest of her committee were going to the children's ward of the hospital to hand out gifts to the patients. They'd planned it for weeks; they'd wear red-and-green hats and be "Santa's helpers."

But first, she'd get to talk to Beau!

When she met Jessica in the hallway, Elizabeth was reminded of their quarrel a few nights before. They hadn't had much to say to each other since.

"I'm sorry about what I said the other night, Jess," she told her sister. After all, she didn't want to spend Christmas fighting with her twin. Three days of silence had been enough.

Jessica's expression was lofty. "Sure," she

muttered. "I knew you didn't mean it. Me—selfish? Who would believe a thing like that?"

Somehow her tone lacked conviction. But Elizabeth was too excited to worry about Jessica now.

Both girls hurried through breakfast. Then Elizabeth and Jessica pitched in to make sure the house was spotless. For once, even Jessica didn't complain about cleaning up.

Elizabeth vacuumed and Jessica dusted, and their mother had fresh-baked Christmas cookies and fruitcake ready, plus eggnog in the refrigerator.

When the house looked presentable, Elizabeth dressed carefully in one of her best sweaters and skirts. But before she could comb her hair, she had to drag Jessica out of the bathroom.

"Hey," Jessica said, protesting. "I'm not finished. I'm trying to decide which color lip gloss to wear."

"I have to comb my hair," Elizabeth told her. "You've been in the bathroom for an hour."

"I have to look good for Beau," Jessica explained. "I want to make a good impression on him."

Eventually, both girls finished getting ready and made their way downstairs, keeping a watchful eye on the clock.

Almost noon, Elizabeth told herself. *Not much longer.* Her mother was upstairs on the phone with a client, but Elizabeth and Jessica were ready to welcome their guest.

Elizabeth put some Christmas cookies out on a plate, along with several slices of her mother's rich fruitcake. She arranged the plates carefully on the coffee table, and plumped the cushions on the couch. She wanted everything to be perfect.

Each time a car passed in the street outside, Elizabeth jumped up and ran to the window to look. Jessica was at her side.

"Just an old Chevy," Jessica said in disappointment. "That can't be Beau."

Elizabeth giggled. She'd almost like to see the young actor pull up in a beat-up old junk heap, just to see her sister's expression.

But the hands on the clock began to creep past the hour, and still no one had pulled into their driveway.

"What can be keeping him?" Jessica asked. "You don't think Lila was right, do you, Lizzie?"

"Of course not," Elizabeth declared, trying to sound confident. "I believe he meant what he said. Beau wouldn't let us down."

But worry flickered inside her, continuing to grow as the minutes passed. Suppose his agent hadn't written down the appointment, Elizabeth thought. Suppose no one had told Beau that Elizabeth had called?

She began to pace up and down the hallway. Surely everything wouldn't go wrong now. But the clock continued to tick. Still no car appeared. Still no Beau.

Jessica looked more and more gloomy as time passed. "I don't believe he's coming," she declared. "He's not interested in us after all. I'm sorry I saw all his movies twice!"

"He wasn't coming to see *us*," Elizabeth reminded her sister. "Beau was coming to help us plan a hospital fund-raiser. I thought maybe we could auction off some of his old costumes, or maybe have a special screening of his new movie, *Tender Hearts*. Oh!"

"What? Is he here? Do you see his car?" Jessica dropped the fashion magazine she'd been reading. She jumped up from the couch, where she'd been sprawled across the cushions.

"No," Elizabeth said. "But I've got to leave for the hospital, to give out the toys. It's almost two. Oh, Jess. I know Beau meant to come. Something awful must have happened."

Jessica shook her head. "He probably forgot all about it," she said darkly. "Lila was right."

"I don't believe that," Elizabeth said, trying

to keep her voice firm. "I think he meant to come. It must have been something really urgent."

"That's exactly what I mean," Jessica argued. "We're just not important enough. I don't like Beau that much anyhow." Pouting, she sank back on the sofa. "See if I ever go to one of his movies again!"

Mrs. Wakefield came down the stairs. "Did your guest arrive yet, Elizabeth?"

One glance at Elizabeth's disappointed expression was answer enough.

"Oh, dear. Well, maybe you'll hear from him later," Mrs. Wakefield said. "Keep your chin up. Come on, I'll drive you to the hospital."

Elizabeth felt like crying. But she refused to believe that Beau was so irresponsible.

"I know he meant to come," she whispered to herself as she followed her mother out to the car. "I just know it."

Six

Jessica heard the kitchen door shut, then the hum of the car's engine as Elizabeth and Mrs. Wakefield pulled out of the garage. As the sound of the car faded away, Jessica paced around the room, then sprawled back across the couch. Frowning, she picked up her magazine. But even the sight of the newest spring fashions didn't help her concentrate on the glossy page in front of her.

How could Beau Dillon not show up, especially after she'd told half of Sweet Valley that he was coming. This was going to make Jessica look stupid in front of all her friends. Lila would never let Jessica live it down.

Jessica shook her head. Maybe she'd lead a picket line in front of the Valley Cinema. She'd march up and down. "Beau Dillon doesn't keep his promises!" her sign would say. His popularity would plummet. Then he'd be sorry he'd let them down!

She heard the sound of a car in the driveway. Had Elizabeth forgotten something? Sighing, Jessica pushed herself up from the couch and went to peer through the front window.

Jessica gasped. A silver-gray limousine had pulled to a stop in their driveway.

"Beau!" Jessica muttered. "I don't believe it. He did come."

Elizabeth and their mother must have just missed him, Jessica thought. As she watched, a uniformed chauffeur appeared from the front of the limo. Before he could open the rear door, a young man stepped out.

Jessica's eyes widened. She'd know that slim, well-built frame and broad shoulders anywhere. She jumped back from the front window before he could see her gawking like some star-struck kid. "Now, what do I do?" Jessica muttered to herself.

She looked around the living room. She ran

to snatch up the magazine she'd left on the couch and shoved it back into the magazine rack. Everything else was perfect, down to the tray of cookies and cake still sitting on the coffee table.

The doorbell rang.

Jessica took a moment to glance at her reflection in the hall mirror. She pushed back a lock of hair, then ran to open the door.

"B—B—Mr. Dillon!" she said. "Oh, I'm so glad you came."

"Miss Wakefield?" Beau Dillon's gray eyes reflected his smile as she nodded. "Call me Beau, please. I can't tell you how sorry I am to be so late," he said.

"That's OK," Jessica stammered.

"We had car trouble after we left my interview, and we had to wait on the highway for a mechanic to come out. Even then, it took him some time to get the limo going again. I tried to call you on the car phone, but your line's been busy for hours."

"Oh, my mom was on the phone," Jessica remembered. "Come in, please."

"I know you must have thought I wasn't coming," Beau told her, his smile rueful.

"Of course not. I knew you wouldn't break your promise," Jessica said, completely forgetting all her earlier grumbling. "Would you like some Christmas cookies? Or some fruitcake?" She offered him the tray.

"Umm, those look good," Beau said. He looked over the tray, then accepted a frosted reindeer and took a bite. "I'm afraid I can only stay a minute. I'm way behind on my schedule because of the breakdown. I have an important meeting this afternoon in Los Angeles. I'm going to be late as it is, but I couldn't go without seeing you first."

"Oh, I can't tell you how much it means to me that you came." Jessica's tone was fervent. Now she'd get to see Lila eat her words, she thought.

Beau nodded. "Yes, I could tell from your letter how much this fund-raising drive means to you," he agreed. "Mainly, I just wanted to tell you I hadn't forgotten about the children's wing of the hospital, and our appointment. What if we meet on the twenty-seventh?"

"Oh, that would be great," Jessica agreed, so excited at the thought of seeing Beau again that she didn't stop to consider the implications of the rest of his speech.

"Fine," Beau agreed. "It's a date. In fact, I'll book a private room at one of the restaurants in town and take you to lunch, to make up for today's disaster. How does that sound?"

Jessica's eyes widened. A *date* with Beau Dillon. Well, sort of a date. Could anything be more wonderful? Lila would turn green with envy.

"I'd love it," she assured him.

"Good, we'll plan the fund-raiser then," Beau assured her. "Now, I have to run. It was a pleasure meeting you, Elizabeth."

"Bye, Beau," Jessica said as he hurried toward the door. "Oh!"

What he had implied earlier finally sank in. Beau thought she was Elizabeth. Of course, why wouldn't he? He obviously didn't know that Elizabeth had a twin sister. He'd been expecting one twelve-year-old girl, and that's what he'd found. Well, Jessica thought, Elizabeth *could* have mentioned her in the letter she'd sent.

"What is it?" Beau paused in the doorway to glance back at her.

"Uh, I hope you don't have any more car trouble," Jessica said quickly.

"Me, too," Beau grinned at her. "See you in a few days. Merry Christmas."

"Merry Christmas to you, too," Jessica called as she watched him get back into his limousine.

She shut the front door slowly, then leaned

against it. She should have told him right away that she wasn't Elizabeth. Now she was starting to feel a little bit guilty. Except she'd been so excited when he actually showed up that she hadn't realized right away the mistake the young actor had made.

And when she did—well, how could anyone be expected to give up lunch with a movie star, especially one as nice and as good-looking as Beau Dillon? Jessica felt her heart beat faster just thinking about it. And they would plan the hospital fund-raiser. Did it matter whether it was Elizabeth or Jessica who did it?

After all, Jessica told herself, it was Elizabeth who said the only important thing about meeting Beau was getting him to help with the fund-raiser. So Elizabeth wouldn't mind if Jessica took her place. Well, not much, anyhow.

Jessica glanced into the hall mirror, trying to pretend that she believed her own arguments. For a moment she almost thought she saw Elizabeth's face reflected there instead of her own. And Elizabeth looked hurt and angry, as if fully aware of her twin's double cross.

Jessica took a deep breath and shut her eyes. When she looked again, she saw only her own face, looking a little bit scared. And as for the lunch date with Beau Dillon—well, it was too much to expect that she confess the whole mistake to Elizabeth now. She'd tell her sister after the luncheon, and let her handle the rest of the details for the fund-raiser. And they'd both get to see Beau during the event itself, wouldn't they?

What she was doing wasn't really that bad, Jessica told herself. But she took care not to glance into the mirror again.

It was almost dinnertime when Elizabeth and her mother returned. Elizabeth came in through the kitchen, her expression anxious.

"Jessica, were there any phone calls for me?"

Jessica shook her head, trying not to see how her sister's expression changed at the answer.

"Well, I know he'll call soon," Elizabeth declared. "I know Beau won't let us down."

"How did the gift-giving at the hospital go?" Jessica asked quickly, hoping to change the direction of Elizabeth's thoughts.

"Oh, it was wonderful," Elizabeth told her sister. "You should have seen the children's faces. We took gifts around to everyone, and they were so excited. One little girl about five—she was in a wheelchair—was so happy with her doll. And they loved our 'Santa's helpers' hats.

Brooke's father put on a puppet show, and we all sang carols."

"Speaking of carols," Mrs. Wakefield said, coming in after Elizabeth, "we'd better get dinner on quickly. It is Christmas Eve, you know. We have to get down to the civic center on time for the concert."

"That's right," Elizabeth agreed. "Handel's *Messiah* is so beautiful. I love it when the choir holds candles as they sing."

"And then we have to decorate the tree," Jessica added. "And sing carols and read Christmas stories. Oh, and I almost forgot. We even get to open one gift tonight!"

The two girls smiled at each other. Christmas Eve in the Wakefield house had its own traditions, and they both loved every minute of it.

"I'll have sandwiches and soup ready in just a moment," Mrs. Wakefield said. "Jessica, I hope you didn't eat too many cookies and spoil your appetite."

Jessica glanced at the tray of snacks, where Beau Dillon had sampled the cookies. "I didn't," she said, knowing that she looked guilty.

Her mother laughed. "Well, Christmas only comes once a year. Come give me a hand in the kitchen, girls."

Most of the family talked and laughed through dinner. Only Elizabeth seemed a little quiet. Jessica found it hard to be as happy as usual. Her big secret clung to the edge of her thoughts.

The choir performance was as moving as always. When the Wakefields got home, Steven and his father put the tree into its stand, and the girls hurried to bring the boxes of ornaments up from the basement. The fragrant scent of the spruce filled the house as the girls discussed who got to hang which ornaments, and just how the decorations should be placed on the tree.

When everyone was done admiring the finished tree, Mrs. Wakefield passed around mugs of eggnog. Mr. Wakefield read the last chapter of Dickens' *A Christmas Carol*, which they had started a week earlier.

Normally Jessica loved the part about the ghosts—it was so deliciously spooky—but tonight she found it hard to listen to her father's calm voice, even with the lights on the tree twinkling softly. Her guilty secret seemed to grow heavier with each passing hour. She could almost feel its weight on her shoulders. She tried to push the thought away, but it just kept coming back.

"Now 'The Night Before Christmas,' " Elizabeth begged. "It wouldn't be Christmas Eve without that."

When Mr. Wakefield finished the poem about old Saint Nicholas, Jessica yelled, "Now the presents!"

"Only one," Mrs. Wakefield admonished. It was a custom at the Wakefield home that on Christmas Eve everyone got to open one of the smaller gifts from underneath the tree. It made it easier to wait for Christmas morning if you had a glimpse of the good things to come, Jessica thought happily.

She chose Lila's gift. She and her friend had exchanged gifts earlier, promising not to open them until Christmas. Well, Christmas Eve counted, Jessica thought. The gift was wrapped in a cylinder of cardboard. She knew it had to be a poster, but she was dying to see which one.

"Maybe it's a picture of Beau Dillon," Elizabeth said as Jessica stripped the paper off the long cylinder.

"Oh, I hope not," Jessica said before she thought. She was trying her best to forget about Beau for a few hours. Her guilt grew heavier every time his name was mentioned.

"Oh, I still think he's going to come through for us," Elizabeth predicted. "I really do."

To Jessica's relief, however, the poster was not of a movie star. Instead, it was of a large, purple unicorn. The animal's head was held high as it tossed its mane, and it had bright, spirited eyes.

"It's beautiful!" Jessica exclaimed. "And so perfect. A unicorn—get it?"

"We get it," Steven said, rolling his eyes. "As if we're not overexposed to your precious Unicorn Club as it is."

Jessica ignored his teasing. "I gave Lila a pair of unicorn earrings," she told her family. "I guess we both had the same idea. Funny, isn't it? I just love my unicorn poster."

Elizabeth had chosen Amy's gift to open. "Oh, the new Amanda Howard mystery," she said happily. "This is great! I've been dying to read this one."

"Seems as if your friends know your tastes very well, girls," Mr. Wakefield observed, grinning. "How about you, Steven?"

Steven had finished unwrapping his present. "Look," he said. "A biography of my favorite basketball star. Terrific!"

They all laughed at his enthusiasm.

"It's been a really perfect Christmas Eve,"

Elizabeth said, her voice soft. "Well, almost. But I still believe in Beau's promise."

Jessica looked away from her sister's hopeful expression. Why couldn't Elizabeth forget about Beau Dillon, at least for a while?

"What's wrong, Jess?" Elizabeth added. "You look awfully gloomy."

"Oh, I'm fine," Jessica said quickly. "Why wouldn't I be?"

Elizabeth shrugged and leafed through her new book.

Jessica tried to pretend she was in her usual high spirits. But she didn't feel as happy and excited as she usually did on Christmas Eve. She felt like a rat!

Seven

After they had opened one gift apiece, all the Wakefields gathered around the tree and sang their favorite carols. Elizabeth laughed when her father and Steven tried to harmonize on "We Three Kings" and Steven made his voice very deep. But Jessica could tell her twin wasn't very happy. Her eyes had a sad, misty look to them.

It's all my fault, Jessica told herself. She felt awful, but she just couldn't think of a way out of her lie now.

"I'm too tired to sing any more," Jessica announced when they came to the last line of "The Twelve Days of Christmas."

"Already?" Steven looked surprised. "Come on, Jessica. Just a few more."

After three more carols, even Steven agreed it was time for bed.

"You'll all want to be up bright and early tomorrow morning," Mrs. Wakefield said, smiling at her children. "And we old people need some sleep."

"Right," Mr. Wakefield said. "You don't want us all to sleep right through Christmas."

"No chance of that," Steven said, heading for the kitchen for one last bedtime snack. "Jessica will be up before six, ready to open all of her presents, just like last year."

Jessica couldn't wait to get upstairs. Every time she looked at Elizabeth it was as if her twin were accusing her with her eyes. She said good night to her parents and immediately trooped up the steps to the second floor with her new poster tucked under her arm. After rummaging through a drawer to find some tacks, she positioned the poster carefully on her bedroom wall, then stood back as she checked to make sure that it hung straight. When she looked into its eyes, Jessica gasped. The unicorn was looking at her—really *looking*! She could see the dark of its eyes as it rolled them, the angry expression as it bared its teeth—

Jessica jumped back, too frightened to scream. She could feel her heart pounding. Even the unicorn knew about her terrible secret!

Then, bravely, she glanced at the poster once more. This time, she saw only the spirited unicorn printed on the page, tossing its mane, its teeth no longer bared in rage.

Jessica covered her eyes with her hands. What was wrong with her?

"Jess, are you all right?" a soft voice asked. "Are you sick?"

Jessica snatched her hands away from her head and whirled toward the voice. It was Elizabeth, looking through the bathroom doorway at her sister.

"Oh, sure," Jessica lied. "I'm fine."

"Why were you covering your eyes?" Elizabeth's expression was puzzled.

"I'm just tired," Jessica told her.

"You look pale."

"I'm OK!" Jessica almost shouted. "Why shouldn't I be? Are you trying to accuse me of something?"

Elizabeth looked startled. "Of course not. Why should I do that? Take it easy, Jess."

Her sister's worried face didn't help Jessica's guilty conscience at all. How could Elizabeth be so concerned about her when she was such a terrible sister? Yet how could she confess her deception to Elizabeth now? Jessica felt worse and worse.

"Better get to sleep. You know we'll be awake by six o'clock at the latest," Elizabeth predicted, smiling. "Merry Christmas, Jess."

"Yeah," Jessica muttered, her tone sour. Elizabeth could easily go off to bed with an easy conscience. *She* hadn't told lies and disappointed her twin.

Jessica brushed her teeth and washed her face, then dropped her clothes on the floor and pulled a flannel nightgown over her head. She climbed into bed, pulling the blankets up and reaching for the lamp on her bedside table.

She gasped. Right before her eyes, the new pink lamp that matched her pink-and-white bedroom wavered. Its outline seemed to quiver, then it dissolved into the old "baby" lamp that she and Elizabeth had used back when they still shared a bedroom. The lamp she saw now was white and yellow, and had a clown's face on the base.

Elizabeth had loved the old lamp, but Jessica always thought that the clown looked as if it were laughing at her. One day, feeling grumpy, Jessica had deliberately pushed the lamp off the bureau, then watched it shatter on the floor. She'd never confessed to breaking the lamp.

Elizabeth had been upset when she found the broken lamp. Jessica had pretended to be sorry, too, hiding her secret pleasure. No one had ever discovered who had really broken the lamp.

Jessica shivered in fright. The clown on the lamp glared at her, and she could almost see the wide, painted lips move.

"Liar, liar!" it called.

Jessica pulled the blankets over her head. It was several moments before she found enough courage to lower the covers and look back at the lamp.

It was pink and rounded again, with a frilly white shade. Her normal bedside lamp. She sat up straighter, frowning. What was wrong with her tonight? She must have eaten too much, she told herself.

Shaking her head, Jessica reached for the lamp again. She hesitated just a moment, almost dreading the darkness, then scolded herself again.

"You're too old to be scared of the dark," Jessica muttered aloud. She clicked the switch on the lamp, and the room was plunged into darkness.

Jessica dove back under the covers. Then, when nothing alarming happened, she laughed at herself. She could hear her parents in their bedroom, the faint sound of their voices as they got ready for bed.

She lay back and waited to drift off to sleep. But tonight was even worse than most Christmas Eves, when she was sometimes too excited to fall asleep. Even after her parents turned off their light, and the house settled down into silence, Jessica lay stiffly in her bed, staring into the darkness.

The house seemed to have gathered a life of its own. Usually she could identify the soft night sounds—the hum of the refrigerator down in the kitchen, the gurgle of water in the pipes as Steven went back to the bathroom for a glass of water, the soft groan of beams settling as night time temperatures dropped outside the house.

But tonight the house seemed to creak and groan as never before. Jessica listened to the noises that seemed to rise and fall all around her, wondering how the rest of the family could sleep through all these ear-splitting sounds.

When she heard soft tapping at her window, Jessica sat up straight in her bed, cold with fear. What was that?

Then she recognized the sound and laughed at herself. It was only raindrops, beating on the windowpane. But the evening sky had been clear—it wasn't supposed to rain tonight.

The last time it had rained on Christmas Eve, she and Elizabeth had been only five. She remembered Elizabeth's crying, afraid that Santa Claus would turn back and not deliver their presents. Their father had had to reassure Elizabeth and Jessica that Santa wasn't afraid of a little rainstorm. If he could brave snow and sleet, Santa surely wouldn't be upset about getting a little wet. And sure enough, on Christmas morning they'd found a wonderful dollhouse under the tree—not even damp—along with scores of other gifts.

Jessica slipped out of bed and tiptoed to the window to look out at the rain. She pulled back her curtain.

But the windowpane was dry. The sky was dark and clear, and a half-moon shone faintly down on her. She saw no clouds, no rain.

How could she have heard raindrops?

More frightened than ever, Jessica hurried back to her bed. Diving beneath the blankets again, she shivered. She must have been dreaming, even though she'd never felt more wide awake.

Would this night never end?

Eventually the stiffness faded from her body, and Jessica forgot to hold her breath and listen for every new and frightening noise. Her eyes closed, and her thoughts wandered.

Then, just as she felt herself drifting off, a sharp sound made her whole body start. She stared into the darkness. The room seemed even blacker than usual—the night light in the bathroom must have gone out. Jessica shivered.

She felt disoriented. What time was it? Jessica turned to look at her digital clock. The blue numerals read *12:00*.

Midnight. The witching hour, when strange things happened.

Jessica felt her bed shake slightly.

Her heart seemed to jump to her throat. Too frightened to shriek, she turned slowly to look. What she saw made her draw back in horror.

A little girl stood at the foot of her bed.

"Who are you?" Jessica gulped.

Eight

The child smiled.

Jessica felt the hair on her neck rise in fright. Her heart pounded so hard that she could almost feel herself shaking.

"Who are you?" she whispered again.

"I am the Ghost of Christmas Past," the little girl answered. Her voice was light and clear. It seemed to hold the tinkling of silver bells within it.

Jessica's eyes narrowed. That name sounded awfully familiar. Was this a trick?

"I don't believe you," she blurted out. "That's a name from one of our Christmas stories. Did Steven put you up to this? Is this one of his practical jokes?"

He'd never pulled a joke this elaborate, but still, it was better than thinking that this terrible vision might be real!

"I am the Ghost of Christmas Past," the child repeated. She sounded very young, and yet strangely old. She frowned slightly. "I am here to take you on a journey through the past."

"Whose past?" Jessica exclaimed, still wondering if this might be some kind of trick.

"Your past," the child said. Her face seemed to blur and then reappear, fading in and out of Jessica's sight. She was dressed in some kind of long white nightgown that shimmered slightly around the edges.

Staring at this vision made Jessica's eyes hurt. She lifted one hand to rub her eyes. She shut them tight, hoping that when she looked again, the strange child would have disappeared.

But when she opened her eyes, the vision was still there. Now the little girl lifted one arm toward Jessica.

Jessica shivered. Beneath the hazy glow that surrounded her, the child's face was somehow very familiar. She had long blond hair, blue-green eyes, and a dimple—

"Why, you look like us!" she cried. "Elizabeth and me. Who are you?"

"I am your younger self, come to help you relive old memories," the child said calmly. "Come."

"I'd rather not," Jessica said hesitantly. But when the child reached across and touched Jessica's arm with her cold fingers, Jessica found herself unable to resist.

"Rise, and walk with me," the child said.

With the child's cool hand clasping her own, Jessica followed the little girl out of bed and across the room. She trembled and felt very cold, but was unable to stop even long enough to grab her robe or slippers.

The child led her straight toward the bedroom window. It was a long drop from the second floor down to the ground. "Where are we going?" she cried out in fear.

"Do not be afraid," the little girl said. "As long as you hold my hand, you will be safe."

As if to prove her statement, the child tightened her grip. The window in front of them seemed to fade away.

Jessica held her breath. But instead of dropping to the ground far below, she found herself drifting through a strange white fog. Voices called out all around her. She could hear snatches of old songs and faint laughter. Jessica shivered and clung tightly to the strange child's hand.

Abruptly the mist faded, and she found herself walking along a path. They were in the park in the center of Sweet Valley. Spring flowers bloomed alongside the walkway, and the air was balmy and warm.

"I know this place," Jessica said slowly. "Lizzie and I used to play here all the time. Oh, there's the old carousel."

Then she stopped. The park authority had torn down the carousel years ago! How could it be standing there again, looking almost new? Its large center canopy was painted red and blue, and the horses looked splendid with silver tassels on their bits and shining manes.

The little girl beside her smiled, as if hearing Jessica's thoughts.

Jessica looked closer and saw two small blond-haired girls, not more than a few years old, each clinging to a horse. They laughed gaily as they circled with the merry-go-round. Cheerful music played, and everyone seemed happy.

"Look!" Jessica cried. "That's us. Oh, Lizzie, can you see me?"

She ran closer and waved to her sister, who was riding on the white carousel horse. Elizabeth was laughing, but didn't seem to notice anything unusual.

"These are but shadows of the things that

have been," the child in the white robe said. "They have no awareness of us."

"You mean they can't see or hear us?" Jessica asked. Sighing, she saw it was true. Little Elizabeth continued to laugh as she rode the white horse. Little Jessica was right behind her atop a spotted pinto. They both waved at their mother, sitting on a bench just beyond the ride.

When the carousel finally stopped, little Jessica slipped off her horse before Mrs. Wakefield could come to help her. She began to beg for a turn on the slide.

"Come and help me, Mommy." Little Jessica pulled on her mother's arm.

"Oh, please. I want another ride on the horsie," little Elizabeth pleaded.

Mrs. Wakefield seemed torn. "All right, once more," she told the small Elizabeth. "Then we'll go to the slide, Jessica."

The young Jessica pouted briefly, but agreed to climb back on her spotted horse.

From a few feet away, Jessica watched her young self and her sister. She felt very glad that Elizabeth had gotten another ride that day.

"She loved that carousel so much," she murmured to herself. "And to think they would ever tear it down."

"Did you say something?" the spirit beside her asked, her voice quiet.

"No, no." Jessica answered. She turned to look at the little girl in white and suddenly felt afraid again. "You really are a ghost, aren't you?"

"Yes," the child answered. "But I mean you no harm. Do not be afraid."

"Why are you here?" Jessica shivered in spite of herself.

"To show you a part of yourself that you seem to have forgotten," the spirit said. "Now come."

She clasped Jessica's hand again, and they moved down the path. They took only a few steps, and the park faded away. Jessica blinked and saw that they were now inside Sweet Valley Elementary School.

She looked around eagerly. They stood just in front of the second-grade classroom. Jessica peered around the doorway, grinning at the sight of the childish drawings pinned to the bulletin board.

"Oh," she cried. "Look, there we are."

A line of second graders came out of the classroom as she spoke, walking more or less quietly to lunch. She saw Winston Egbert, in a brand-new striped shirt—he couldn't seem to stop twirling a button—and little Lila Fowler in a characteristically stylish dress, her brown hair sleek and pretty. And there was Amy Sutton, tall even in second grade, her blond hair in pigtails.

But most of all, Jessica stared at herself and her sister.

They were dressed in identical outfits, pink denim jumpers and white T-shirts. Elizabeth had her hair pulled back and pinned with white ribbons, Jessica had her hair down and wore one big pink bow at the top of her head. They both wore white knee socks and pink tennis shoes.

"We used to always dress the same," Jessica murmured. "I'd almost forgotten how much fun we thought it was to look alike."

The two small twins were whispering furiously to each other.

"Didn't you love that story in reading today?" little Elizabeth whispered to her twin. "About Ali Baba and the forty thieves?"

Little Jessica nodded. "Yes. And you read aloud better than anybody in class," she told her twin loyally. "I thought you were the best. I'm glad Mrs. Becker gave you a gold star for your chart."

"She should have given you one, too," Elizabeth said. "I thought you were just as good!"

"I giggled too loud when Winston made a face at me," Jessica reminded her twin. "I don't care about gold stars, anyhow."

"You can have mine," Elizabeth promised.

"Boy, Mrs. Becker wouldn't be too happy about that." Little Jessica giggled at the thought.

"Hey, Jessica," Lila Fowler called from up ahead. "Come walk to the lunchroom with me. I'm in the front of the line."

But Jessica shook her head. "I'd rather stay with my sister," she called back.

Lila looked disappointed.

The teacher turned to frown at them. "Quiet, children. Let's walk nicely to the lunchroom."

Jessica sighed, watching the line of children march obediently off. Would she have turned down Lila's invitation today? Probably not. Something inside her ached a little, to see the twins so happy and best friends. What had happened to that special kind of friendship and trust?

Now they had moved inside the lunchroom. Jessica saw little Elizabeth and the younger version of herself sitting down at a table, side by side.

"Oh," little Jessica said, clearly upset. "They forgot to put a chocolate chip cookie on my plate and it's my favorite."

"Don't worry, Jess," Elizabeth told her sister. "We can share mine."

"She's always so good to me," Jessica told the spirit beside her. "Lizzie loves chocolate chip cookies. She didn't have to split that with me. I'd forgotten all the times she's done nice things for me."

"Really?" The spirit regarded her closely.

Jessica was once more absorbed in the scene before her. Elizabeth broke her cookie in two pieces and reached across to give her twin the bigger piece. Little Jessica smiled, putting one arm around her sister's shoulder to give her a quick hug.

"Ha, ha," someone called from the next table. "Look at the second-grade babies!"

Both girls turned to look. It was Bruce Patman, sitting with a group of third graders. Elizabeth frowned at him, but Jessica jumped up from her bench. She advanced upon the older boy, looking so fierce that he drew back.

"Don't you dare talk about my sister!" she yelled. "Or you'll be sorry, Bruce Patman. Pat Man the Fat Man—so there!"

Bruce wasn't really fat, but he turned red. The boys sitting around him laughed, and he seemed to lose interest in teasing the girls. He turned his back on the Wakefield twins.

Jessica came back to her table and took her seat beside her sister.

"That was great, Jess," Elizabeth told her sister, her tone admiring.

"Nobody better talk about *my* sister," Jessica said darkly. She lifted her chin. "Or they'll have to answer to me."

The little girl was so protective and yet so childish that Jessica had to laugh. Yet, inside, she felt a great sadness. How good it had felt to see herself stand up for her sister, and how proud she was of her younger self.

What had happened to that Jessica? When had she begun to change?

The Ghost of Christmas Past reached out to take Jessica's hand again.

Jessica winced at the coldness of her touch. "Do we have to leave already?" she asked.

"Not yet." The spirit still held Jessica's hand in a firm, cool grip.

Jessica looked up to see that the elementary school had disappeared. Now they stood in the hallway of the Wakefield house, just at the foot of the stairs. But Jessica's home didn't look quite the same as usual. What was different?

"There's that old vase that Steven broke trying to dribble a basketball in the house," Jessica remembered. "And that rug is the one Mom replaced two years ago. I know where we are, but *when* are we, spirit?"

Instead of answering, the spirit nodded toward the stairs. Jessica heard a rush of small feet, accompanied by a storm of giggling. Then she saw her smaller self, still seven years old, hurrying down the staircase, with young Elizabeth right behind. Both little girls wore long pink-and-white flannel nightgowns beneath their pink robes.

Little Elizabeth called over her shoulder, "Hurry up, Mom, Dad. Steven, we beat you downstairs!"

Jessica followed the two little girls eagerly into the living room. The spirit remained close beside her. It was great fun to see the little girls pounce on their Christmas stockings with excited squeals, examining the small toys and treats stuffed inside.

"Hurry up, so we can open the presents," little Jessica yelled.

The pile of gifts beneath the tree was really impressive. Little Jessica couldn't take her eyes from the pile of boxes wrapped in green, white, and red, and Elizabeth looked just as impressed.

At last Mr. and Mrs. Wakefield arrived, following a sleepy-eyed Steven into the room. Mr. Wakefield had his camera ready as Mrs. Wakefield began to hand out the gifts.

Then what a flurry of opening gifts—the paper ripped and the ribbons flew! How much fun they had!

Steven exclaimed over a brand-new basketball. "Boy, just what I needed!"

He *hasn't changed much*, Jessica told herself.

Little Jessica and Elizabeth got identical red velvet dresses with white lace collars. They had to stop everything to try the new outfits on, then look at themselves in the hall mirror.

Jessica giggled at the sight of the little girls admiring themselves.

There were still more gifts. Some were identical—two small tea sets of pink-and-white plastic dishes—and some were slightly different. Elizabeth opened a coloring set, and Jessica had a makeup kit. Slowly the great pile of gifts began to dwindle.

Jessica leaned over her younger self, watching as the little girl unwrapped a sweet-faced baby doll, dressed in blue and white.

"Oh, she's so cute," Elizabeth said. "I have one almost the same, but I like yours better."

Hardly glancing at the doll that her twin held, little Jessica picked up her new doll and thrust it at her sister. "Here then, we'll switch," she said gaily.

"Oh, Jess, are you sure?" Elizabeth looked doubtful.

Jessica was firm. "Of course," she said. "This is Christmas. I want my best friend to be happy."

Mrs. Wakefield gave the little girl a hug. "What a fine example of the Christmas spirit," she said. "I'm proud of you, Jessica."

Elizabeth joined the hug. "Me, too," she agreed. "You're the best sister anyone could ever have, Jess."

Watching this scene, Jessica felt very small and empty inside. Would she do the same thing today?

Somehow, she knew the answer was no.

"Is something the matter?" the spirit beside her asked.

"No," Jessica said hastily. "Nothing, except —oh, I don't know."

She thought briefly of the carousel horse that Elizabeth had liked so much. Had Jessica really wanted the horse as much as her sister? Or had she simply been selfish?

Jessica felt the emptiness inside her grow.

Then she realized that she no longer felt the clasp of the spirit's cold hand. She reached out, touching nothing but vacant space.

"Spirit?" Jessica called. "Where are you?"

Nine

◇

Jessica found herself sitting up in her bed, back in her own bedroom. She looked around wildly. But everything looked normal. The blankets on the bed were smooth. Only her new poster on the wall was missing—where had the poster gone?

Jessica heard the clock in the hall downstairs strike one. One o'clock! What was she doing awake in the middle of the night? And she had had such a strange dream—it had been a dream, hadn't it?

Jessica shivered. The house was very quiet; no more grunting and grumbling, no more strange bumps and knocks. But she had never felt so alone, as if she were the only person in the house.

What a terrible thought! Jessica shuddered again and tried to control her imagination. She thought about the dream; had it really been just a nightmare?

Jessica sat up straighter and looked all around her bed. She was afraid she might discover another strange figure sitting on the end of her mattress. But she saw nothing unusual.

Taking a deep breath, she bent over the edge of the bed and lifted her bed ruffle. Nothing under her bed but a few balls of dust and several old magazines.

"You're being a real scaredy-cat," Jessica told herself. "Go back to sleep. It was only a dream. Nothing else is going to happen."

But how could she sleep when the light was so bright? And who had left the light on in her bedroom?

Jessica's heart plunged to the pit of her stomach. It wasn't her bedroom light at all; neither the ceiling light nor the pink lamp beside her bed was switched on.

Instead, a strange, white light glowed from the hallway. It was so bright, so intense that just the trickle of it beneath her bedroom door lit up her whole room. Jessica could hardly bear to look. She had to squint and hold up one hand to shade her eyes. What could it be?

Somehow the idea of waiting for that door to open seemed even worse than confronting the unknown. Jessica pushed her blankets aside and felt for her slippers. She edged off the bed, her knees wobbling as she approached the door. She forced herself to touch the doorknob, almost feeling the strange energy coming from the other side of the door. At the very last moment, Jessica thought about diving back into bed and hiding her face, but an eerie voice called faintly from the hallway. *"Jessica?"*

Jessica felt a chill run through her whole body. She tried to answer the summons, but her voice wouldn't work. She cleared her throat and reached for the doorknob again, turning it slowly.

When she pulled the door open, the light outside was blinding. Throwing up her hand, she could barely open her eyes enough to see.

Blinking, Jessica stepped into the hall. But this didn't look at all like their usual upstairs hallway. Instead, it reached on and on, and the bright light flowed from some unknown source farther down the long corridor.

As Jessica walked forward, she moved away

from the safety of her bedroom. The hall seemed to stretch on endlessly. At last she came to a large window.

She hesitated, not sure whether to approach and look outside. The window suddenly flew up—all by itself—and a great rush of night air lifted her hair and made goose bumps rise all over her skin. Jessica shrieked.

Through the open window, a cold wind swirled and a magnificent purple unicorn galloped into the room.

"Oh!" Jessica gasped. "Who are you?"

The unicorn dropped to the floor, pawing the carpet and tossing its head. "Who am I?" It seemed insulted. Its deep voice echoed with the rich sound of distant trumpets. How fierce the animal's expression was, and how long and sharp was the silver horn on its forehead!

"I'm sorry, but I don't know who you are," Jessica explained in a small voice. She tried hard not to show her fear.

"I am the Ghost of Christmas Present," the proud animal said. "You shall know me better."

Jessica wasn't really sure she wanted to. As she looked closer at the beautiful creature, she saw sprigs of holly and mistletoe caught in its thick mane. Its body glistened, almost as if it were lightly dusted with stars. And its midnight-blue tail was so long and so thick, it seemed ready to brush the sky.

"Come, get on my back," the unicorn ordered. "We have a journey to take together."

To Jessica, the unicorn was much scarier than the sweet-looking little girl who had taken her on a journey through her past. She didn't want to go for a ride on the unicorn's back. She wanted to race down the hall back to her cozy bedroom. She wanted to snuggle under the covers and wait for Christmas morning.

"I can't. I'll fall off."

"Get on," the unicorn ordered, in a deep, booming voice. The creature lowered its head, and the silver horn glowed menacingly.

"I'll try," Jessica said, trying to hold back her tears. She approached the great beast cautiously. She wasn't sure how she managed to scramble up, but she found herself on its back. The unicorn felt cold as she pressed her cheek to its neck. She wrapped her fingers through the thick mane and clung tightly.

The unicorn took a great leap forward, and the hall disappeared. Now they were charging through white fog. The air was cold and damp. Yet, now and then she caught a glimpse of clear stars beyond the mist.

Jessica clung even tighter as the unicorn

galloped through the fog. She felt her slipper slide off her right foot and fall, lost at once in the billowing mist.

-    Jessica thought about what would happen if the unicorn decided to throw her off its back. She would plunge endlessly to some terrible doom. Sobbing, Jessica quietly prayed that she wouldn't fall.

The unicorn galloped lower, and now Jessica could make out lights coming from houses in the distance. Some of the houses were large and splendid, some small and modest. But all were decorated for Christmas, with colored lights glinting through the windowpanes.

The unicorn tossed its head and bounded forward. The next thing Jessica knew, they landed in a spacious yard carefully landscaped with lush plants and trees. Water in a large blue swimming pool looked cool and serene amid the greenery. A wooden deck jutted out from the house beyond, where vast expanses of glass reflected the peaceful scene. On the deck, relaxing in casual slacks and a knit shirt, sat a handsome young man.

"Beau Dillon!" Jessica cried. "This must be his house. I've seen pictures in the fan magazines. Oh, thank you, spirit, for letting me see Beau again."

The unicorn snorted. Was the animal angry? Jessica swallowed any more exclamations. She could hear Beau talking to another man, who was sitting in the next chair.

"It made me feel good," the young actor was saying, "to see someone that young able to care so deeply about other people. I really enjoyed meeting her."

Jessica leaned forward. Was it possible Beau was talking about *her*? Had she really impressed him? She smiled in delight.

"So concerned about the sick children in the hospital. And so certain I would show up and not let her down. She's a sweet girl, not like the spoiled brats we see sometimes. It will be a pleasure to help Elizabeth raise money," the young movie star explained.

The two continued to talk, but Jessica wasn't listening any longer. *Elizabeth*, Beau had said. And if he'd really met Elizabeth as planned, everything he said would have been true.

But instead, Jessica thought miserably, it was all a lie. She couldn't even enjoy the young actor's good opinion of her, because it wasn't really her he was praising.

Oh, why had she ever thought that lying would be worth the risk? Jessica bit her lip, trying not to cry.

With no warning, the unicorn leapt forward again. She clung to its back as it galloped once more through the clouds.

Jessica didn't mind leaving the young movie star's home. It wasn't fun seeing him or listening to him talk about her, not when he thought she was really Elizabeth. Why had Jessica ever allowed Beau to go on believing his mistake?

Where were they going now? The unicorn was dropping to earth again. Jessica strained to see through the white mist. What she saw made her eyes widen with happiness.

Ten

◇

"I'm home!" Jessica told the unicorn. "This is my house."

But somehow she knew she wasn't yet permitted to slide off the unicorn's broad back. So she sat very still, looking over the Wakefields' living room.

The Christmas tree lights twinkled. All the decorations had been so lovingly made and selected, it made Jessica feel warm inside. The huge pile of gifts beneath the tree caused her to realize that it was now Christmas morning.

"There we are," she told the unicorn, watching Elizabeth and Steven hurry into the room.

No, it wasn't Elizabeth. It was her, Jessica. And why did this vision of the room seem a little strange, a little blurred and out of focus?

"You are seeing this scene through your sister's eyes." The unicorn's deep voice rumbled close to her ear. "You will be able to hear Elizabeth's thoughts, feel what she is feeling. Something you haven't done lately."

Jessica felt her guilt well up inside her again. How did the unicorn know everything that had happened? She glanced at the beast doubtfully. For just an instant the unicorn paled, its horn faded away, and she saw in its place a giant white carousel horse, just like the one she and Elizabeth had quarreled over.

"Oh!" Jessica cried. She shut her eyes tightly. When she dared to open them again, the unicorn stared back at her. The expression in its blue-black eyes seemed accusing.

Jessica looked away. She tried to pay attention to the merry scene before her. The two girls were opening gifts, arguing cheerfully with their brother, while Mr. Wakefield snapped pictures with his camera and Mrs. Wakefield passed around presents.

"What a pretty sweater, Jess," Elizabeth said now. "It's almost the same shade as my new slacks."

"Don't think you can borrow it," her sister warned, her tone sharp. "It's brand-new, after all."

Jessica felt herself turning red. Why did she have to be so hateful to her twin? She felt sick to her stomach.

"Can't I tell myself to behave better?" she begged the unicorn.

The animal shook its head.

The worst part was that although Elizabeth chattered and laughed as usual, something felt wrong. With Jessica's new perception, she could feel that Elizabeth wasn't really as happy as she seemed.

"What's wrong?" Jessica asked the unicorn.

"Look inside her," the beast said.

Jessica tried to read her sister's deepest thoughts. *I was so sure that Beau would come,* Elizabeth thought. *I still can't believe he let me down. I really trusted him. I'm going to disappoint all my friends. Some fund-raiser I turned out to be.*

"Oh," Jessica moaned. "I didn't think she was this upset!"

"Perhaps she didn't want to spoil the whole family's Christmas," the unicorn suggested.

Jessica didn't answer. *That sounds just like Elizabeth,* she thought crossly. So noble. Why couldn't her sister just come right out and admit she was miserable?

"It's not my fault that I didn't know she was unhappy. Am I supposed to know things she won't tell me?" Jessica complained.

"Are you her sister, her twin?" the unicorn's deep voice asked. "Her best friend? Don't you know her better than anyone else in the world?"

"You mean I *should* know her better than anyone else," Jessica said slowly. "You're telling me I've been too selfish again, right?"

The unicorn lifted its ears at her question, but didn't answer.

Jessica focused her thoughts on Elizabeth again. Something else was making Elizabeth unhappy. What else was wrong?

I keep thinking that Jessica is involved in this somehow, she could hear Elizabeth thinking. *She won't look me in the eye, and she seems preoccupied. I don't know why, I just have this feeling . . .*

Jessica shuddered. Her sister was too close to guessing the truth! And if Elizabeth discovered what had happened, would she ever trust Jessica again? Would she ever love her completely again, as she had when they were younger, when they were more as sisters should be?

"Why was I so selfish?" Jessica wailed.

"It wasn't worth it, not for Beau, not for any movie star. Not if it comes between Elizabeth and me!"

"A little late to decide that, isn't it?" the unicorn asked.

"I don't know," Jessica sobbed. Tears ran down her cheeks and onto the unicorn's thick, purple mane. "Please tell me she'll forgive me and still love me. I've only got one sister. Please help me, unicorn. I'm not usually mean to my sister."

Instead of answering, the unicorn leapt upward so suddenly that Jessica had to cling desperately to it to keep from falling.

The clouds seemed even thicker now, and their borders were shadowed with darkness, as if a storm were brewing. A sharp flash of lightning broke through the night. Jessica screamed.

Then a clap of thunder rolled and rumbled all around them. Jessica's ears rang with the terrible noise. She hugged the unicorn's neck with all her might, too frightened even to sob. When they finally headed back to earth, everything seemed to whirl around her.

Jessica squeezed her eyes shut. When she opened them, she was surprised to see that they were back in the Wakefield home. But no Christmas decorations shone on the windows, no holly adorned the hall mirror. Where were they? Or *when* were they?

What had the unicorn brought her to see?

Jessica saw Elizabeth come into the den. She looked like her normal, sixth-grade self. She had schoolbooks and a notebook under her arm, but the notebook looked shiny and new.

It was the beginning of sixth grade, Jessica guessed. And Elizabeth had been crying. What could have made her sister so unhappy?

"Mom, can I talk to you?" Elizabeth asked.

Mrs. Wakefield looked concerned. She closed the door to the den and gave her daughter her complete attention.

"Jessica wants to be a Unicorn," Elizabeth burst out. "And she kept it a secret. She doesn't tell me anything. We never do things together anymore. And she doesn't even care!"

Elizabeth cried, her whole body shaking.

Watching, Jessica swallowed, trying to rid herself of the uncomfortable lump that had formed in her throat. She remembered her own high spirits at the first of the school year, how excited she'd been about joining the Unicorns.

"But is this something *you* would like to do, Elizabeth?" Mrs. Wakefield asked her daughter.

"No," Elizabeth said, and wiped her eyes. "I'd only join to be with Jessica. It's not really the club, I guess. It's just that Jessica and I don't do everything together anymore, and now Jessica doesn't even want me around."

"I'm sure that's not true," Mrs. Wakefield said. "And although I know you miss her, it is good for you both to have separate interests, Elizabeth."

Mrs. Wakefield tried to comfort her daughter, while Jessica watched.

Elizabeth had never told her sister how unhappy she'd felt when Jessica began to do things on her own. She'd put on a smile, as usual, and agreed that they should have friends on their own, do different things.

Jessica had never, until now, known how miserable she had made her twin.

"Oh, Lizzie." Jessica felt the scene before her blur as her own eyes filled with tears. "I'm sorry I made you unhappy, honest I am."

"Too late," the unicorn rumbled. It took another great leap, and Jessica cried out in fear. "Please stop!"

But the creature ignored her cries, continuing to climb. It soared higher and higher. Jessica's head spun, and she was afraid of what was coming next. This time, she was sure, the unicorn would drop her. She'd fall to the ground far below and shatter like a broken doll.

The unicorn snorted and plunged so wildly that no matter how tight she clung to its neck, Jessica could feel herself beginning to slip. With one last great leap, the unicorn sprang out of her grasp. Jessica began to fall. The cold mist rushed past her.

"Help!" Jessica cried.

Eleven

◇

Jessica sat up with a jerk. She was back in her own bed again! She discovered that she was breathing hard, and shaking with fright from her fall. Had she really fallen through the clouds? Was it only another dream?

Jessica pulled the covers up to her chin, trying to breathe normally. Enough was enough. All she wanted was for this terrible night to be over. Then Christmas morning would come, and everyone would be happy again.

Everyone? Jessica thought of Elizabeth, hiding her secret sadness, and sighed.

What was she going to do? What about Beau Dillon and the lie she'd told? Jessica pushed the thought away. Not now, not in the middle of the night.

Jessica glanced at the clock on her bedside table. It was almost two o'clock. Surely she could sleep this time without any more terrible visions.

She glanced around the room. Everything looked normal. The curtains at her window hung as usual, with no cold wind to stir them. The unicorn poster was on her wall, where she had put it, and there was no strange light coming from the hallway.

Jessica felt sure that her wild dreams had ended.

She lay back in bed and closed her eyes, willing herself to fall asleep. At first her body felt tense and stiff, but gradually the tension began to fade. Jessica thought how nice it was to feel the soft mattress beneath her, the thick blankets over her to keep her warm. The sweet scent of flowers—

Flowers?

Jessica felt her body stiffen all over again. She didn't have any fresh flowers in her bedroom. Then, to her bewilderment, Jessica felt something hard poking her in the back, as if her almost brand-new mattress had developed lumps. What was going on?

Jessica opened her eyes. Pale afternoon sunlight made her blink in surprise. She touched the surface beneath her and found that she was lying on a smooth carpet of grass. Well, not completely smooth—she pushed a small rock out from under her back. Rubbing the sore spot through her nightgown, Jessica sat up. She looked around, confused.

Where was she?

Somehow, she had gotten to a small field of grass and flowers, surrounded by a thick grove of trees. It looked almost like the forest beyond Secca Lake, where she and her family sometimes picnicked and hiked. But there was no sign of any footpath. Jessica felt her heart beat faster. Was she lost?

She walked hesitantly toward the trees. Deep shadows lay beneath the tall evergreens, and the undergrowth was thick and tangled. It was not an inviting place to wander alone.

Maybe she should just stay here, Jessica thought. But as she was thinking about it, the sunlight began to fade and the shadows deepened. The sun was setting, Jessica realized, although the tall trees hid the rosy sunset from view. If she stayed any longer, she wouldn't be able to find her way back at all, wherever that might be.

Jessica shivered, glancing uneasily at the dark patches inside the trees. She didn't want to walk through that shadowy wood. She might get hopelessly lost. Worse, she was afraid of what she might see.

But what choice did she have? Glancing around the small glade one more time, Jessica took a deep breath and plunged into the forest.

It was even darker beneath the trees than she'd imagined. She had taken only a few steps when she stumbled over a root. "Ouch!" Jessica muttered. She stopped to rub her sore toe—why did she always end up on an adventure without her slippers?—then she pushed on.

The darkness grew more and more intense. She had walked only a few more feet when she scratched her ankle on a brier. "I don't like this," Jessica complained out loud. "I want to go home."

No one answered. Sighing, Jessica pushed forward through the trees. How long had she been wandering through the forest? It seemed like hours.

"This is ridiculous," Jessica grumbled. "What

am I doing here? What am I supposed to see? I'm not a forest ranger."

Then a chill ran over her back. Jessica stopped abruptly, wiping the beads of perspiration off her face. She suddenly had the feeling she wasn't alone. Was someone watching her?

Jessica turned quickly, her eyes narrowing as she searched all around her. But the dark forest held its secrets, and she could see nothing out of the ordinary. The thought of strange eyes watching her secretly made Jessica shudder.

"If you're there, come out!" Jessica yelled. "Why can't I be allowed to see you?"

She waited for an answer. But although she strained her ears, all Jessica could hear was the slight murmur of the wind in the treetops, a night bird singing, and the faint, faraway chatter of a chipmunk.

Then the bird song stopped suddenly, and the chipmunk dove under cover. Even the wind seemed to die.

Jessica caught a faint flicker of movement from the corner of her eye, and she whirled around.

She was sure she was going to faint. She could hardly breathe.

A figure stood half-hidden beneath the shadow of the tallest tree. It was tall and thin, and she could hardly make out the outlines of its form.

Jessica shivered. Why did it stand so still? Why didn't it speak?

"Are you the third ghost?" Jessica demanded, nervousness making her voice sound shrill. "Have you come here to guide me?"

The strange form glided forward. Jessica took a step backward before she could stop herself. The form was tall, but still hard to see clearly. It was draped in a white, loose-fitting robe that covered it from head to toe, with a deep hood that gave no glimpse of the face within the shadows.

Jessica's heart was pounding so hard it made her dizzy. She had never felt so alone. "You're worse than the other two," she blurted out, clutching the thin sapling beside her to steady herself. "Much worse. But I know you're here for a reason. Are you the Ghost of Christmas Yet to Come? Are you going to show me what my future holds?"

The figure's head moved very slightly, nodding beneath its oversized hood.

Jessica took a deep breath. Her knees were still wobbly and weak.

"All right then," she agreed. "Lead on, spirit, and I'll follow."

To her relief, the spirit turned to the right, instead of coming any closer. It moved between the trees silently, and Jessica had to hurry to follow its noiseless footsteps.

At least the walking was easier now. The spirit seemed to know the easiest path, and Jessica made her way with less stumbling.

At last they emerged from the forest. They were standing at the edge of Secca Lake. Its water gleamed dark and still under the night sky. A bonfire burned brightly on the sandy shore of the lake, and a group of teenagers was gathered around the fire.

Jessica lifted her tired shoulders. It was good to leave behind the dark and frightening forest. She hurried forward to approach the group. The white-robed spirit stayed at the edge of the trees, standing silently within their shadow.

Jessica felt some of her fear fade away. The teenagers were laughing and talking together. At the center of the group, Jessica saw a slim girl in stylish clothes. She had blue-green eyes, long blond hair, and a dimple in her left cheek.

"It's me!" Jessica shrieked, delighted with this glimpse into her future. Then she covered her mouth with one hand, glancing nervously at the group of boys and girls standing so close.

But none of them seemed to hear her. She felt sure they couldn't see her, either. Jessica forgot to worry and took another step closer.

What a gorgeous teenager she would grow up to be, Jessica thought happily. Pretty, well dressed, cheerful, obviously very popular. Boy, had Elizabeth ever been wrong in her prediction that Jessica wouldn't have any friends.

"I just love your sweater," one of the other girls said. "Where did you find it?"

"The new boutique in the mall," the older Jessica said. "I'll be happy to show you next weekend."

"I wish." The other girl sounded wistful. "But I've spent all this month's allowance, and my mom said absolutely no more advances. We've got our big sorority party coming up, too. I guess I'm out of luck."

"One of my neighbors needs a baby-sitter this weekend," Jessica's older self suggested. "I was going to do it, but if you need the money, I could recommend you for the job instead."

"You're really a good friend," the second girl said with a smile. "Thanks."

"Hey, Wakefield," one of the boys called. "Come here and help us with the marshmallows. We need your expert touch."

"As if you can't burn them all by yourself."

The blond girl laughed. "Don't worry, I'm coming." She picked up a plastic bag of marshmallows and moved closer to the fire.

Jessica watched her older self help the boys skewer the marshmallows on pointed sticks and hold them over the leaping fire. She grinned as she saw how the boys all maneuvered to be close to the blond girl, without being too obvious about it. They all made jokes and teased her in a good-natured way.

The older Jessica answered each one with a quip, ready to laugh and tease them back.

"Oh, I knew Elizabeth was wrong," Jessica told herself, delighted with this vision. "I knew I'd be as popular as ever when I grew up."

She saw her older self glance once or twice at the dark forest.

Jessica bit her lip. Could the older Jessica somehow see the silent spirit, which still stood in the shadow of the trees?

But the older girl seemed to have someone else on her mind. "I hope our—uh—initiate is doing OK," she murmured. "It's awfully dark in the forest. You're sure you guys left the white tags in plain view so she can find the trail back to the lake?"

The boy she turned toward just shrugged. "Sure," he said easily. "I know the rules."

The older Jessica nodded, looking relieved. "We need to put the hot dogs on now," she decided. "I'll get them out of the van. And we need some more soft drinks. Hey, guys, I need some help with the coolers."

"Sure thing," the first boy agreed. Two more boys hurried to help her.

Jessica grinned, watching her older self walk away toward the van, out of sight beyond the trees. Several boys tagged along to help. As the blond teen walked away, Jessica heard a murmur from the group that remained around the campfire.

"Poor thing, to have such a witch for a sister," one of the girls whispered. "How can they look alike and yet be so different?"

"Yeah," another girl agreed. "Can you imagine that creep of a sister thinking we'd allow *her* to join our sorority?"

"Ha, fat chance," another girl laughed. "You're sure she'll never find her way out of the woods in time?"

"Are you kidding?" a boy answered. "I put those white tags so high on the trees she'll never see them. She's going to fail the initiation; that way she'll never be able to join."

"Thank goodness," the first girl said.

Jessica backed away from the bonfire, feeling a little sick. What had happened to make Elizabeth so unpopular? Sure, her sister could be a bore, always worrying about homework and her stupid school newspaper. So she liked to help other people, working on charity drives. But Elizabeth had always had friends, always been well liked at school. What could have gone so wrong?

Some of Jessica's pleasure at seeing her older self had faded. Why hadn't the older Jessica done something to help her unpopular sister?

"Was that what you brought me to see?" she called to the spirit. "But I'm trying to get Elizabeth into the sorority. She—I mean, I—can't know that the other kids aren't playing fair."

The spirit didn't answer. But it lifted one hand to beckon.

Reluctantly, Jessica followed as it turned and stalked away. She didn't want to leave the cheerful campfire, but how could she argue with a ghost? She walked slowly back into the dark forest.

Farther and farther into the trees they went. Now the woods seemed even darker and more frightening. Small noises sounded around them, making Jessica's hair crawl on the back of her neck. The shadows seemed to move and flicker for no reason.

Jessica wished she'd never followed the ghost back into the woods. Could she possibly find her way back to the lake by herself? Just then a new sound met her ears, like a very faint whimper.

Jessica stopped abruptly. Did she hear someone crying?

Twelve

Jessica plunged wildly through the woods, heedless of the damage to her bare feet. The air was cold on her face, but she had to keep running. She was sure that she had heard her sister's voice. Jessica couldn't bear to hear that hopeless sobbing. Where was her sister? She had to find her.

The darkness was so intense that she lost the path and ran smack into a tree trunk.

"Oh!" Jessica cried.

The impact made her bend over, gasping with pain. For a few moments she couldn't move. Then she caught her breath and straightened.

Had it stopped? Had she lost the faint sounds she'd been following?

Jessica listened for the sound of crying. No, there it came again. Pushing the tree branches out of her way, Jessica hurried forward.

Finally she followed the sound of the sobs to the shadows beneath a large tree. At the foot of the tree, curled up into a miserable ball, huddled the teenaged Elizabeth.

She looked dreadful even in the very dim light. Her hair was a mess, with broken twigs caught in its tangles. Her legs were scratched, and she'd torn her sweater. Her eyelids were swollen and her nose was red from crying. Big tears still ran slowly down her cheeks as she sobbed angrily.

Jessica felt terrible. "It's going to be all right, Lizzie," she said. "I'll help you somehow with the other kids. Don't cry!"

But the blond teenager continued to sob. Jessica remembered that her sister couldn't hear her. What could she do? She began to walk up and down in front of the other girl, feeling powerless and frustrated.

The teenager huddled on the forest floor muttered to herself. Jessica stopped pacing and leaned closer to make out the words.

"Oh, Elizabeth," the girl murmured. "How

could you let them treat me like this? I know they're all spiteful, but I didn't expect this of you."

Jessica looked at her in horror.

But the other girl didn't see her. "I didn't even have a chance at passing this initiation. Those white tags weren't anywhere to be seen—I looked hard, honest. The girls just don't want me to join the sorority. And the boys are helping them make sure I fail the test."

Jessica stood still, motionless with surprise and horror as the girl's first words hit home. *Elizabeth*, the girl said?

Jessica bent to peer more closely at the angry, sobbing girl. The trees above them swayed in the wind. A silver shaft of moonlight slipped through the treetops, and Jessica was able to see the girl's face more clearly.

Her eyes were swollen from crying, and the girl was too angry for her dimple to show. But her hair was worn loosely around her face. And— Jessica suddenly remembered—the girl at the bonfire had had her hair pulled back, just like Elizabeth always did.

This miserable reject was Jessica!

Jessica bit her lip to hold back her own tears. How could this be? Only a few years from now, and Elizabeth was the popular, pretty one, while Jessica ended up alone and unhappy.

This couldn't be right, Jessica told herself. How could such a thing happen?

Elizabeth's voice sounded in Jessica's memory: *"If you keep on being so selfish, you'll end up with no friends at all."*

Jessica shut her eyes, blocking out the unwelcome sight in front of her. "I don't believe it," she muttered.

The wind in the treetops was her only answer.

Jessica stamped her bare foot, her voice rising. "I don't believe it! That can't be me!"

She felt a wave of dizziness and reached out to steady herself by grasping a tree trunk.

The tree wasn't there. The forest had vanished, and with it the sobbing girl. Now Jessica stood at the edge of a football field. She recognized the Sweet Valley High School stadium. A football game seemed to be under way.

Jessica turned to look beside her. She shivered to see the silent ghost in its white robe standing all too close. She inched away from the frightening specter.

"What am I supposed to see here?" she asked. "That miserable girl wasn't really me, spirit, was it? Tell me it's not true."

The ghost raised one arm. Its hand was invisible, lost in the long white sleeve, but Jessica knew that it was pointing.

Jessica turned to look at the edge of the football field. A group of girls moved in practiced rhythm, leading a cheer. Jessica recognized many of the same girls from the bonfire. They were all pretty and full of spirit. One of the girls had dark hair and dark eyes, and she moved with special animation.

"Who's the best?" she yelled. "S-W-E-E-T V-A-L-L-E-Y! That's who!"

As the rest of the team shouted, the crowd in the bleachers cheered with them.

"Go, Cara!" a boy in the stands called. "That's the spirit. We've got the best cheerleaders, as well as the best football team."

The cheering squad moved swiftly into a pyramid. Jessica watched them climb with practiced ease onto the bottom girls' shoulders.

"Boy, they look good," Jessica told herself. "I could have done that."

The girls finished their cheer, then tumbled gracefully to the ground. The crowd cheered loudly.

Jessica felt a sharp stab of envy.

"*I* should be out there with them," Jessica muttered. "That's the kind of teenager I should have become. I've always wanted to be a cheer-leader!"

She felt cheated, as if all her dreams had faded away right before her eyes.

"I wish you'd never brought me here," Jessica told the ghost. "I feel awful. How can I go home now, knowing what's going to happen to me?"

But the spirit only continued to watch the scene before them.

Jessica looked through the crowd. Toward the front, she noticed the blond teenager who Jessica had thought to be her older self. The girl sat with a group of lively teenagers, all laughing and talking as they watched the game.

On the field, Sweet Valley made a touch-down. The blond teenager jumped up, cheering along with her friends.

Now that she saw the girl under the bright lights of the stadium, Jessica could see the re-semblance to Elizabeth. This girl had pulled her blond hair back from her face. The erect way she held herself reminded Jessica of her sister, also. There was no doubt which twin this was.

"But where am I?" Jessica cried.

She looked around to locate the ghost again.

The white-robed figure stood a few feet away, in the shadow of the bleachers. For an instant, Jessica wondered how the cheering people in the stands weren't able to see the frightening sight.

And although she couldn't detect a face beneath the large, drooping hood, Jessica knew that the ghost's eyes were fixed on her. Trying not to think about her fear, she spoke to the spirit.

"Surely I've got to be here somewhere?" she pleaded. "All the high school kids are at the game, having fun. Where am I?"

Once more the spirit raised its hand in a silent gesture. Jessica turned away from the field. Her glance scanned the crowded bleachers.

Every time she found a knot of giggling, talking girls, Jessica narrowed her eyes. She tried to make out her older self. She surveyed every girl with blond hair closely, but without luck.

At last she spied a solitary figure at the far side of the bleachers. This girl sat on the top plank, all alone. Her shoulders were hunched over, and she had no one to talk to, no one to laugh with. She didn't even have enough energy to yell and cheer for the team.

"Oh, no." Jessica bit her lip. "Spirit, that can't be me."

She hurried forward, anxious to see the lonely girl more clearly. The girl on the bleachers wore a stylish outfit; her skirt and sweater were perfectly matched, and her hair was expertly groomed. She looked lovely, just like the kind of girl who would be appreciated and liked by the other high school students. What had gone wrong? Why was she sitting here all alone?

Jessica seemed to have extra-sharp hearing—perhaps it was the ghost's presence. She could hear a group of girls down the bleachers whispering to each other.

"Serves her right, sitting all alone. She's been so hateful," one of them said, as she reached for a handful of popcorn.

"She's so self-centered," another agreed. "Poor Elizabeth. Can you imagine having to put up with a sister like that?"

Jessica blinked hard, trying not to cry. It *was* true, then. That isolated, unhappy girl was her older self, and she had absolutely no friends.

Jessica climbed onto the bleachers—she seemed lighter than air—and bent closer to the two girls.

"What did Jessica do to *you*?" she begged them. "Why do you dislike her so?"

The two girls continued to giggle.

Jessica bit her lip. Of course, they couldn't hear her, not in this ghostlike state.

But she seemed able to influence their

thoughts a little. Or was it just coincidence that the first girl said, "Once I actually wondered if Jessica might be fun to be around. But I remembered all the gossip—how selfish she is, and how she only thinks about herself."

"That's right." The second girl nodded. "People still talk about that trick Jessica played on Lois Waller, remember, when she put the shaving cream on her sundae? And that was years ago."

"Yeah, but she's been doing mean stuff like that ever since. Remember the time when she tried to steal Todd Wilkins from her own sister? That was so selfish."

"Right. And how about the time that Elizabeth wrote to Beau Dillon, and Jessica pretended to be Elizabeth just so she could meet him," the second girl said. "I mean, a movie star like Beau!"

Both girls made faces. "That was a totally rotten thing to do," the other girl added. "How could anyone trust a person like that?"

"But I didn't mean it," Jessica cried, desperate to wipe that disgusted look off their faces. "I'm going to fix it, honestly. I changed my mind."

But the girls were chattering now about an upcoming dance at school. Jessica Wakefield suddenly seemed very far from their thoughts.

Jessica scrambled back to the bottom of the bleachers. Maybe some mistakes couldn't be fixed, she thought. Maybe her future really was going to be this awful.

The spirit waited for her in the shadows, still silent. A chill ran through her every time it glanced at her. She felt totally defeated.

"I can't bear this," she told the ghost. "I want to go home."

She squeezed her eyes shut, and felt a wave of dizziness wash over her.

"Please take me home!" Jessica begged.

Thirteen

◇

When the cold mist no longer touched her face, and the swirling air receded, Jessica opened her eyes. She hoped she would find herself back in her bedroom.

Instead, she was at a restaurant booth. There were bottles of ketchup and mustard on the table. Wide-eyed, Jessica looked around. She knew this place. It was the Sweet Valley High crowd's favorite hangout, the Dairi Burger. Jessica and her Unicorn friends from the middle school also liked to spend time here.

If this was the future, the place didn't seem to have changed much, Jessica told herself. But it obviously was Christmastime. Candy canes decorated the counter, and a slightly lopsided tree sat in the corner. And there was even fake snow covering the windows.

Jessica quickly lost interest in the decorations. A noisy group of teenagers caught her attention. She stood up and walked closer to the front of the restaurant. Did she know any of these people?

Of course! Jessica recognized some of the faces. The students might be older, but they still seemed very familiar. Lila Fowler's brown hair was neat and stylish, and she wore an expensive cashmere sweater. Next to her sat Bruce Patman and another boy. All of her old friends from the middle school were here, Jessica told herself, frowning. But where was she?

In the next booth sat—no, not herself—Elizabeth again, looking cute and perky in a miniskirt and blue sweater. She was surrounded by friends—Olivia Davidson, Winston Egbert, and Todd Wilkins, plus a whole crowd of boys and girls Jessica didn't recognize.

Everyone seemed to be having fun. They all laughed and talked as they exchanged small Christmas presents. Jessica saw Elizabeth grinning as she opened a pile of gifts.

"Oh, a fountain pen," she exclaimed. "It's beautiful. Todd, I love it."

It was obvious that Elizabeth was the center of the group, Jessica realized. She felt a pang of envy as she watched her pretty, happy sister. As Elizabeth brushed back her blond hair, Jessica saw a gold bracelet on her arm, with a lovely gold heart dangling from it. It was the very same bracelet she and Elizabeth had seen in the mall when they were window shopping, Jessica realized. *Probably one of Elizabeth's many friends bought it for her*, Jessica thought with a frown. Elizabeth was exactly the picture of the poised, attractive teenager Jessica had always hoped to become. The teenager she *should* have become!

Where was her older self?

Jessica backed away from the noisy groups of teenagers, looking toward the back of the restaurant. Who else was here?

Two girls sat silently at nearby tables in the very back of the snack bar.

Jessica hurried closer to take a look. The first girl was Lois Waller, still overweight, still looking lonely and out of place. At the table across from her sat the older Jessica. Today she looked as well dressed and pretty as ever, but the perfectly applied makeup couldn't disguise the spiteful droop to her mouth, or the malicious glitter in her blue-green eyes. Once in a while she shot nasty glances toward the other students.

"Good grief," Jessica muttered to herself. "Why am I sitting all alone?"

As if in answer, Lois looked up and called in a timid voice, "Jessica, would you like to sit with me?"

"Sit with a loser like you?" The teenaged Jessica rolled her eyes. "You must be joking."

Lois flushed and looked away. She was obviously hurt by this cruel rebuff.

"She was only trying to be friendly," Jessica called out, wishing she could shake her older self. "How can you be so mean?"

But the older Jessica didn't answer. The two girls continued to sit alone at their separate tables. They didn't talk. Lois studied a textbook as she slurped her milk shake through a straw. Jessica drank a cola while she flipped idly through a movie magazine; she seemed determined to ignore the other girl.

"Oh, this is terrible," Jessica muttered again. "Spirit, can't we do something?"

The ghost stood a few feet away, motionless in its white robe. It seemed to create its own dark pool of shadows. Still and silent, it refused to answer her plea.

Across the room, Jessica saw the teenaged

Elizabeth and her group get up, waving their goodbyes to the other kids as they left the Dairi Burger. The door banged behind them.

After Elizabeth's group went out, Lila Fowler whispered, "Now, Bruce. Do it now. She deserves it, after the way she treated my cousin last week. Give her a taste of her own medicine."

Jessica's hearing still seemed especially sharp. Lois and the teenaged Jessica at the far table hadn't heard Lila's whisper.

Jessica had a strong feeling of foreboding. What were Bruce and Lila up to?

Bruce Patman left his booth and walked toward the tables where Lois and Jessica were sitting. Both girls looked up at him in surprise. This was obviously not an everyday event.

Bruce pulled a chair up to Jessica's table and flashed her a sparkling smile. "Mind if I join you?"

"Look out, Jess," Jessica tried to warn her other self. "He's up to something. I'm sure of it."

But the teenaged Jessica seemed too surprised to expect trickery. "Oh, sure." She smiled sweetly up at him. "Be my guest."

"You probably don't know it, but I've had my eye on you for a while," Bruce told the blond girl. "I mean, you're really something, Jessica."

Somehow, the teenaged Jessica didn't seem surprised. She seemed to expect admiration from one of the most eligible boys in the high school. "I'm glad you noticed," she murmured.

"Sure." Bruce smiled again. "How could I miss noticing a girl like you?"

Jessica heard a suspicious undertone of sarcasm in his words, but her older self didn't appear to notice.

"In fact, I thought maybe you'd like to go out this weekend," he said.

The teenaged Jessica smiled with pleasure. "A date? I think I could fit you into my schedule."

"There's a dog show at the park on Saturday," Bruce told her.

"A dog show?" Jessica blinked. "You like dogs?"

"Sure—doesn't everyone? Sounds like fun, huh?" Bruce asked, his tone smooth.

"Sure," the older Jessica agreed quickly.

"Good," Bruce said. He stood up. "About two-thirty, OK?"

Jessica nodded. "I'll be ready."

Bruce raised his voice so the rest of the crowd in the Dairi Burger could hear. "I'll send you the number of the booth."

Jessica looked confused. "Booth? Do I need a booth to go to the dog show?"

"To enter you do," Bruce said loudly. "I mean, what better place for a dog like you?"

He threw back his head and exploded with laughter. The rest of his crowd at the front of the snack bar joined in.

The older Jessica's face flushed bright red, and she looked down at her lap, clenching her hands into fists. Tears welled up in her eyes at this public humiliation, and her pain and anger were evident.

Lois Waller looked sorry for the other girl, but didn't seem to know what to do to help her.

Bruce seemed tickled with the success of his trick. "A dog like Jessica, get it?" he repeated for the benefit of his friends.

As their laughter continued, Jessica jumped to her feet and ran toward the door. It banged behind her.

"I can't bear this," Jessica moaned. "Is this the way my future has to be?"

Still the spirit was silent. Its white-robed form seemed to stare back at her, but offered no answer.

Jessica blinked hard, trying to hold back her own tears. What a future to look forward to!

"I don't want to see any more," Jessica said. "You must take me home, please!"

Fourteen

The Dairi Burger whirled around her. The normal sounds of teenagers talking, the aroma of hamburgers cooking, the feel of the smooth tile floor beneath her feet—it all seemed to retreat into the distance.

Jessica shut her eyes, trying not to be overcome by a wave of nausea. She felt the touch of the cold mist on her face again, heard snatches of strange voices floating in and out of the fog. And once—she shuddered at the sound—she heard a girl crying.

The sobs were heart-rending.

It sounded like Elizabeth. Or was it Jessica

herself, alone and friendless because of her self-ish ways? Jessica tried to call out to the un-known person who was weeping, but she couldn't seem to make her voice heard. She tried to see, but the strange fog blurred her vision. The sound of the sobs floated farther away. Once more she was lost in the pale mist.

Then the whirling slowed. When she opened her eyes, Jessica looked around her.

Was she home? Relief flooded through her. Thank goodness!

There was the familiar hallway, with the tall mirror in its regular spot, reflecting the pol-ished, smooth wood of the table on the other side. It sure looked like the Wakefield house. Had the spirit done what she'd asked? Was this terrible journey over?

Remembering the fearful specter, Jessica looked around. The white-robed ghost stood as silently as ever only a few feet away.

Jessica shuddered. "Now what?" she asked. "What are we doing here?"

The spirit lifted one arm and pointed toward the second floor.

That was her answer.

Jessica turned and slowly began to climb the stairs. But instead of heading toward her own bedroom, she found herself being drawn to another doorway. The door was shut, and she hesitated. Should she knock? Would anyone hear if she did?

Then her eyes widened in shock as she found that she could walk right through the doorway. *Just like a ghost*, Jessica thought.

She glanced around at the familiar room. It was blue and white, and the bed was neatly made with pretty pillows and stuffed animals piled high. Shiny trophies sat atop a crowded bookcase, while awards and plaques crowded the walls. Jessica stepped forward curiously to read some of them.

The girl who lived in this room was president of the Pi Beta Alpha sorority, as well as a member of the high school honor society. She'd won awards for writing and for citizenship. In fact, there didn't seem to be much she hadn't done.

Snapshots of friends lined the dresser mirror, signed with affectionate greetings.

Jessica sighed. Not much doubt which sister these awards and photos belonged to. The whole room reflected a happy, busy life. In fact, when Jessica turned, she saw a blond teenager sitting before a large desk on the other side of the room. Elizabeth, of course.

What was her sister doing? Finishing her

homework to get more good grades, or writing a long letter to one of her many friends? Jessica couldn't help feeling bitter. Knowing that her sister couldn't see her, Jessica stepped forward to peer over her shoulder.

No, it wasn't homework or a letter. Elizabeth was writing in a journal. What could she be writing, Jessica wondered idly. A list of her many accomplishments? Or was Elizabeth gloating that she had turned out to be such a popular, accomplished teenager, while her sister was such a loser, all alone and without any friends?

Jessica bent down closer to read the journal on the desk, and instantly she felt a distinct shock.

"I try to be happy," Elizabeth had written. "I have so much to be thankful for—my parents, my friends, the good times at school. But nothing makes up for Jessica's being unhappy."

Jessica blinked in surprise. Did it really matter to Elizabeth, with her own popularity, that her sister was miserable? She read further.

"Worst of all," Elizabeth had written, "I've lost my best friend. Jessica and I don't share anything anymore. We've lost that special feeling we used to have. Being sisters, being twins— that used to mean so much. It was the best feeling in the whole world. I always thought nobody would be able to take it away from us."

Jessica straightened. She looked around the room, knowing that the silent spirit wouldn't be far away.

Sure enough, the white-robed figure stood in the corner of the room. She rushed closer to speak to it, too distressed to remember to feel afraid.

"What happened to us?" Jessica demanded, her tone urgent. "Tell me who came between us. What happened to the happy little girls on the carousel? We loved doing things together, sharing our toys and our snacks. Elizabeth and I cared about each other, even when we were very little.

"And in sixth grade, when we started doing different activities, when we had our own friends, we were still *sisters*. There was still that special feeling, that love the two of us shared. What happened, spirit? You must know!"

But the ghost made no answer. It lifted the white-draped arm again, motioning her back toward the girl sitting in front of the desk.

Jessica felt strangely unwilling to look, almost afraid of what she might learn. But she forced herself to turn back toward the desk. She leaned over her sister once more and skimmed the journal entry.

"I think it began with the terrible trick Jessica played years ago. It was the Christmas I had hoped to meet Beau Dillon," Elizabeth had written.

Jessica felt as if someone had given her an electric shock. Oh, no! Not the awful mistake with Beau again. Well, maybe it hadn't been a mistake. Maybe it was her lie that had led to this. She looked down and read more of the journal entry.

"Jessica pretended to be me, when she knew how badly I wanted to meet him. It was so important to me to persuade Beau to help. Jessica didn't care about the hospital drive—she just wanted to have lunch with a celebrity. And the lunch was a disaster.

"When Beau realized that the fake Elizabeth wasn't really interested in the hospital fundraising after all, he decided not to help. The whole hospital drive was a failure.

"Jessica was forced to tell me, and I was so disappointed. I felt sure that children suffered because we didn't do our part to raise the money for the medical equipment they needed.

"How could I forgive Jessica after that? Besides, one lie always seems to lead to another. I just felt I couldn't trust her anymore. If you don't trust a person, how can you love her?"

The words seemed to blur on the page.

Jessica took a deep breath and rubbed her eyes. She felt frozen inside, almost too numb to feel pain. But the hurt was there, waiting to overwhelm her. She felt anger at herself, and a deep sorrow. How could she have done it? *She* was the one who had pushed the twins apart, through her own selfish actions.

"Oh, Elizabeth," she sobbed. "I didn't mean it. Can't you forgive me?"

She saw that Elizabeth was also crying, pushing away her tears with an impatient gesture. Even with her many friends, her honors, and her activities, Elizabeth was unhappy, too.

And all because of her, Jessica.

What could she do? Was it too late? Had what she'd already done set the future on an irreversible course?

Surely this awful future could still be changed. Jessica ran back to confront the silent specter standing in the shadows in the corner of the bedroom.

"I'll be a different person," Jessica begged. "I've learned a lot. I'll try not to be so selfish— honest I will. Please tell me that this can be changed—that this doesn't have to be my future."

The ghost stared back at her, its face enveloped by the hood.

"You've got to tell me!" Jessica shrieked.

"Say something. Give me a sign. Promise me that the future can still be changed."

But the spirit remained silent. It seemed motionless beneath the white cloak.

Jessica felt her frustrations overwhelm her. She was desperate! She stepped forward, reaching out to grasp the white robe. If she had to, she'd shake an answer from the stubborn ghost.

"Tell me!" she demanded.

It was like touching ice. She gave a sharp jerk on the white robe, and it moved in her hand.

Jessica felt a chill of pure horror run through her. The robe was slipping. What terrible creature would she see lurking within the cloak?

She stared, her eyes wide, as the hood fell away. The face—how awful was it—what would she see?

Nothing. Beneath the white robe was thin air. The white cloak dropped to the floor, and there was nothing beneath.

Jessica let out a bloodcurdling scream.

Fifteen

The cloak seemed to have developed an evil life of its own. Jessica fought frantically against it as it covered her face, wrapped itself around her throat, and nearly choked her.

Jessica shrieked and tried frantically to push it away.

As she wrestled with it, she felt something slip beneath her. She turned around and saw her pillow, lying across the edge of the mattress.

She was back in her bed! Jessica looked at the white cloth that lay tangled around her. She had been fighting with her sheet! She drew a deep breath and tried to relax. She wasn't sure whether to laugh or cry. Pale early morning light shone around the edges of her shade. The night was over at last, and with it her terrible dreams.

What time is it? Jessica wondered. Had she missed Christmas?

The clock beside her bed read 8:05. Jessica never slept this late on Christmas morning.

Pushing the sheet aside, Jessica jumped off the bed, eager to get downstairs. Where were her slippers? She found the left one, but its mate seemed to be lost. Then Jessica remembered how her right slipper had dropped off and fallen through the clouds when she rode the unicorn's back. *No, no*, she told herself firmly. *That was only a bad dream.* Her slipper had probably been kicked beneath the bed.

As she picked up her robe, she caught a glimpse of the unicorn poster on the wall. For just an instant, the unicorn seemed to wink at her.

Jessica stared hard and blinked her eyes. But the poster was just a poster again.

Never mind. Jessica put on her robe and hurried for the door. She could hear voices coming from downstairs.

"Where is Jessica?" she heard her mother saying. "Why is she sleeping so late?"

"I'll check on her," Elizabeth said.

Jessica heard her sister coming up the staircase. She ran to the head of the stairs to meet her. "Oh, Lizzie," she cried, hugging her sister tight. "I love you so much!"

Elizabeth looked surprised, but she hugged her sister back. "I love you, too, Jess," she said. "Merry Christmas."

Elizabeth's blue eyes looked clear; she didn't suffer from a guilty conscience, Jessica told herself. And she did still love her twin, but would she feel the same way when Jessica confessed her terrible lie?

"Funny," Elizabeth was saying. "I glanced into your room before I went downstairs, but I thought your bed was empty. I thought you'd gone down without me. Then you weren't downstairs either."

Jessica shivered. "My bed was empty?"

Elizabeth shrugged. "I guess you must have snuggled so far down into the sheets I just didn't see you," she suggested. "I mean, you just woke up, didn't you?"

Jessica nodded. "Sure, that must be the answer." But a slight chill lingered. Had any of her dreams been real?

Elizabeth turned back toward the staircase. "Come on, Jess," she urged. "We're ready to open the presents. Dad has his camera all set, and Steven's getting impatient."

"Just a second," Jessica begged. "I've got something I need to tell you."

"Right now?"

"Yes," Jessica said firmly. Would Elizabeth still smile at her sister when she heard Jessica's confession?

"It's something I should have told you before," Jessica began.

Elizabeth raised her eyebrows.

Jessica almost lost her nerve. "It's just, I mean . . ." Her voice faded. How could she do it? But she had to tell the truth. The longer she waited, the harder it would be, and the more damage her lie would cause. Hadn't she seen that already in her glimpse of the future?

"It's just—at least now it'll be a Christmas surprise," Jessica hurried on. "Beau Dillon did come yesterday, Lizzie."

"What?"

"He had car trouble. That's why he was late. He only stayed a minute, just long enough to say that he'll be back on the twenty-seventh. He'll take you to lunch and discuss the fundraiser. He still wants to help—that's the important thing."

"He did come? He didn't let me down?" Elizabeth's eyes were wide. "Oh, I'm so happy. Thank you, Jess. What wonderful news!"

Jessica waited for her sister to become angry, to demand to know why Jessica hadn't told her the news earlier. But Elizabeth seemed more happy than suspicious.

"Wait till I tell Amy and Julie," Elizabeth sighed. "Now I know our fund-raiser will be a success. I won't have to feel like a failure after all."

"You, a failure?" Jessica was so surprised, she forgot to worry about her own guilt. "Believe me, that will never happen. I know."

She nodded wisely, remembering the happy, busy teenager she'd seen in her sister's future.

Elizabeth grinned. "How come you know so much this morning?"

Jessica bit her lip. There was no way she could explain the crazy dreams she'd had. Surely they were only dreams! But she'd learned something from them nevertheless.

"Lizzie," she said, her tone earnest. "I'm not always very nice. You were right. I am selfish sometimes, and it will probably happen again. But I'm going to try to do better. Maybe I can be a nicer person, part of the time at least. Just don't forget that I really love you. You're my twin sister, and nobody will ever take your place."

Elizabeth's blue eyes glistened. She seemed genuinely moved by her sister's words. "Oh, Jess, you know I love you, too, no matter what. And I'm sure nothing could ever come between us."

Nothing except my own selfishness, Jessica told herself. *But I will try to remember!*

"Come on. Let's get downstairs, or they'll think we've been kidnapped by Santa." Elizabeth giggled.

If you only knew, Jessica thought, but she didn't say a word. She just wanted to forget her eventful night and enjoy Christmas morning.

The girls hurried down the stairs. Mr. Wakefield's camera flashed as they ran into the living room.

"It's about time," Steven complained. "I want to open my gifts."

"Merry Christmas, sleepyhead," her mother said, kissing Jessica on the cheek. "Are you finally awake and ready for Christmas morning?"

"Definitely," Jessica said, hugging her mother and her father, and then Steven. Her brother looked at her in surprise.

"What's that for?"

"I'm just so happy to see you!" Jessica exclaimed. "I mean, well, Merry Christmas!"

Everyone laughed.

"Christmas is wonderful," she told them, smiling at her family.

"Boy," Steven marveled. "What's with Jessica? She's in an awfully good mood."

"She's got the Christmas spirit, that's all," Mr. Wakefield said, grinning at his daughter.

For an instant, Jessica shivered, remembering the three spirits who had visited her. Had it been in her dreams or did it even matter?

"Are you cold, dear?" her mother asked. "You should have put on your slippers. My goodness, how did you scratch your ankle?"

Jessica glanced down at her bare feet. Sure enough, she saw the red marks on her ankles and legs. It looked as if she'd been on a long walk through a thorny forest. Jessica felt cold again. "On some thorn bushes," she muttered. "It doesn't matter. Oh, is that for me?"

She accepted a large, gaily wrapped package from her mother. "I wonder what it is."

The rest of the Wakefields laughed. "That's more like the old Jessica," Steven teased.

But Jessica heard the fondness in his voice, and she grinned at him as she tore into the package.

When she shook the paper free, Jessica gasped. It was the beautiful carousel horse! Jessica glanced up and saw Elizabeth watching her. Jessica knew exactly what she wanted to do.

"Here, Lizzie," she said. "This is really for you. I know how much you liked it."

Elizabeth looked shocked. "What do you mean? This gift was for you, Jess."

"I want you to have the horse," Jessica told her, "because you're such a special sister."

Elizabeth's eyes widened. "Are you sure? I mean, you liked the carousel horse, too."

"Not as much as you did," Jessica said, determined to be honest. "I know this is very special to you. I remembered the carousel in the park, how we used to ride when we were small. You loved the carousel and its horses. So I want you to have this."

Elizabeth smiled broadly. She accepted the white horse, then hugged her sister again. "This really is special, Jess. How can I thank you?"

"You don't have to," Jessica told her. She looked around the room and smiled at them all. "Having a family who loves you is better than a whole roomful of presents."

"My, my." Mr. Wakefield raised his dark eyebrows. "You certainly are feeling philosophical this morning."

"Here you are, Jessica," Mrs. Wakefield said. "Your turn again."

Jessica accepted another package from her mother and pulled a particularly pretty sweater out of the wrapping. Did it look a little familiar?

"That's pretty, Jess," Elizabeth observed,

stopping her own unwrapping to glance at her sister's gift.

"You can wear it any time you want," Jessica said firmly.

Elizabeth looked at her in surprise, and everyone else laughed. "I think we should have Christmas every day," Steven observed. "Besides all our presents, it seems to put Jessica in an awfully generous mood."

Jessica knew her cheeks were turning red, but she only laughed with the rest of her family. Today she couldn't get angry at anyone.

Everyone laughed and talked and opened gifts until there was nothing left under the tree except a pile of empty boxes and lots of tissue paper.

The girls had new clothes to admire, and games and books to examine. Steven received a new electronic basketball game, which he immediately hooked up to the television and demonstrated to the rest of the family.

Mrs. Wakefield opened a large box containing a beautiful brown leather coat. She modeled it for them all and gave her husband a big hug to thank him.

Mr. Wakefield received ties and cologne from his children, and a new putter from Mrs. Wakefield.

"Just what I needed to take at least three strokes off my golf game," he commented, grinning.

After Mr. Wakefield had taken several rolls of pictures, he finally put his camera away. Mrs. Wakefield passed around a plate of blueberry muffins. No one seemed interested in going into the kitchen to eat a real breakfast.

It's a perfect Christmas, Jessica told herself. Everyone was truly happy. And she knew that Elizabeth no longer had to be sad about Beau Dillon.

Thank goodness I finally decided to tell the truth, she thought with relief.

"Oh," Mrs. Wakefield exclaimed. "I almost forgot. This came by special messenger last night. I don't know which of your friends is so extravagant, Elizabeth."

She brought a small white box out from the far side of the tree and handed it to Elizabeth.

Elizabeth looked surprised. She accepted the package and began to unwrap it.

"Hurry up," Jessica urged. "I want to see what's inside."

First Elizabeth found a note on top of the box. She opened it carefully and read the contents out loud.

"Dear Elizabeth," the note said. "I'm so

sorry about our mishap yesterday. If you're still interested, I look forward to meeting with you over lunch at the Valley Inn at noon, December twenty-seventh. I'm sure we'll come up with a way to give the children at the hospital just what they need."

"It's signed, 'Beau Dillon,' " Elizabeth said in awe.

"Open the box." Jessica jumped up and down with impatience. "Wow, a present from a real movie star."

Somehow, Jessica didn't feel jealous. Instead, she was happy for her sister. It was a wonderful feeling.

Elizabeth lifted the lid of the small white box. She drew out a slim gold bracelet. A gold heart-shaped charm dangled from it.

"How pretty," Mrs. Wakefield said. "And how thoughtful of him, Elizabeth."

"Boy, that must have cost a bundle," Steven pointed out. "This guy's got class."

"He must be a really nice young man," Mr. Wakefield added.

Only Jessica was silent. This was the bracelet she'd seen in her vision of the future! It was true, then. Except now, thankfully, she was certain her future was going to be much brighter than the one she had glimpsed in her dream.

"Jessica, don't you like it?" Elizabeth asked, seeming to misinterpret her sister's silence. "Don't feel left out. I'll let you wear it sometime."

Jessica shook her head. "No," she said firmly. "This is for you, Lizzie. You deserve it. You're my extra-special sister."

Elizabeth smiled, and they hugged each other. "You're special, too," she said. "I'm so happy we'll always have each other."

Jessica laughed, knowing Elizabeth was right. Nothing would ever come between them. They would always have each other, and Jessica felt like the luckiest girl in the world. This was surely the best Christmas ever.

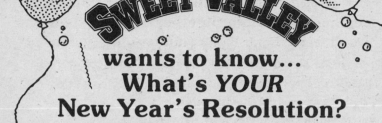

wants to know...
What's *YOUR*
New Year's Resolution?

Announcing
the Sweet Valley
New Year's Resolution Contest!

How are you planning to start the 1990s? Sweet Valley wants to know! And entering our contest is so easy. Just send us a short description of your New Year's resolution (50 words or less). If yours is judged one of the top ten resolutions, you can win:

A copy of your
favorite Sweet Valley book,
autographed by Francine Pascal!

Start the countdown to 1990 and great reading *now*! Send your resolution and your favorite Sweet Valley book title to:

> BANTAM BOOKS
> DEPT. SWEET VALLEY NEW YEAR
> 666 Fifth Avenue
> New York, NY 10103

Entries must be postmarked and received by December 15, 1989. See the Official Rules on the next page!

Good Luck and Happy New Year!

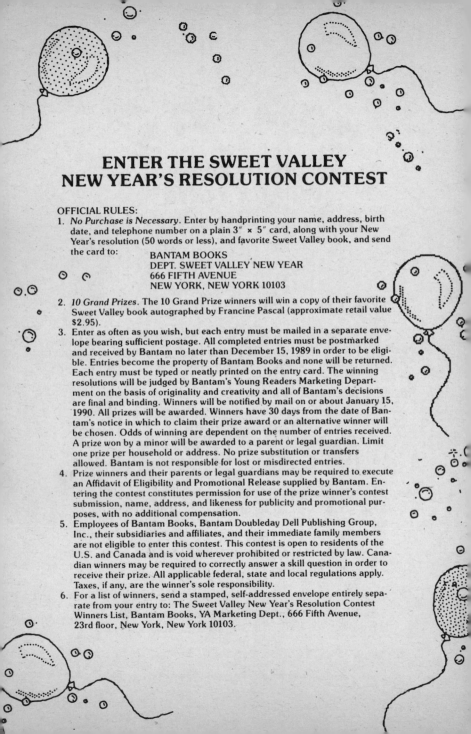

ENTER THE SWEET VALLEY
NEW YEAR'S RESOLUTION CONTEST

OFFICIAL RULES:

1. *No Purchase is Necessary.* Enter by handprinting your name, address, birth date, and telephone number on a plain 3″ × 5″ card, along with your New Year's resolution (50 words or less), and favorite Sweet Valley book, and send the card to:

   BANTAM BOOKS
   DEPT. SWEET VALLEY NEW YEAR
   666 FIFTH AVENUE
   NEW YORK, NEW YORK 10103

2. *10 Grand Prizes.* The 10 Grand Prize winners will win a copy of their favorite Sweet Valley book autographed by Francine Pascal (approximate retail value $2.95).

3. Enter as often as you wish, but each entry must be mailed in a separate envelope bearing sufficient postage. All completed entries must be postmarked and received by Bantam no later than December 15, 1989 in order to be eligible. Entries become the property of Bantam Books and none will be returned. Each entry must be typed or neatly printed on the entry card. The winning resolutions will be judged by Bantam's Young Readers Marketing Department on the basis of originality and creativity and all of Bantam's decisions are final and binding. Winners will be notified by mail on or about January 15, 1990. All prizes will be awarded. Winners have 30 days from the date of Bantam's notice in which to claim their prize award or an alternative winner will be chosen. Odds of winning are dependent on the number of entries received. A prize won by a minor will be awarded to a parent or legal guardian. Limit one prize per household or address. No prize substitution or transfers allowed. Bantam is not responsible for lost or misdirected entries.

4. Prize winners and their parents or legal guardians may be required to execute an Affidavit of Eligibility and Promotional Release supplied by Bantam. Entering the contest constitutes permission for use of the prize winner's contest submission, name, address, and likeness for publicity and promotional purposes, with no additional compensation.

5. Employees of Bantam Books, Bantam Doubleday Dell Publishing Group, Inc., their subsidiaries and affiliates, and their immediate family members are not eligible to enter this contest. This contest is open to residents of the U.S. and Canada and is void wherever prohibited or restricted by law. Canadian winners may be required to correctly answer a skill question in order to receive their prize. All applicable federal, state and local regulations apply. Taxes, if any, are the winner's sole responsibility.

6. For a list of winners, send a stamped, self-addressed envelope entirely separate from your entry to: The Sweet Valley New Year's Resolution Contest Winners List, Bantam Books, YA Marketing Dept., 666 Fifth Avenue, 23rd floor, New York, New York 10103.